A THIRD OPTION

Other Writings by Eugene A. Kelly

For What It's Worth: A Guides For New Stockbrokers (1985)

For What It's Worth: A Guide For New Financial Advisors (2001)

The Pendulum Letters (1990–2019)

Under The Name E. Aly

107 Secrets To Success For The Graduate (2019)

For What It's Worth Essays (2019–)

Change Happens But Will They Understand? (2021)

Three Questions (2021)

19 Rules For Getting Rich And Staying Rich Despite Wall Street (2022)

A Third Option

E. Aly

Marshwinds
Press Company

ISBN 978-1-7341170-5-9 (Hardback)
978-1-7341170-6-6 (Paperback)
978-1-7341170-7-3 (Ebook)

Library of Congress Control Number: 2022919214

Subjects: FIC027000/Romance General; FIC042120/Christian Romance; FIC044000/Women

Book Club virtual readings and Q&A sessions are available by contacting:

Marshwinds Press Company
P. O. Box 21099
St. Simons Island, GA 31522
1-800-343-3751
OR go to www.uniquereads.com
Printed in the United States of America

Cover & Interior Design: Olivia Croom Hammerman Design, LLC

*For Judy,
who makes it all possible.*

A THIRD OPTION

Chapter One

A taxi turned right onto Tenth Avenue from Seventeenth Street and rolled to a stop at the corner of Eighteenth, in front of a decrepit brown and tan building with La Luncheonette 1988 painted on the front. A medium-height, slender woman in her late twenties with shoulder-length auburn hair emerged from the taxi. She wore a light gray, tailored suit with a white blouse, a choker-length string of black pearls, matching earrings, and a delicate gold chain with a gold locket. A black Ricky bag was hooked over her shoulder. Looking around, she stood elegantly erect. Her calf muscles, accentuated by her four-inch-high black Ferragamo pumps, appeared to have been sculpted by a discerning artist. Amy saw Tom, her roommate and lover, crossing Tenth Avenue and assumed the slight smile she wore when first meeting a client in her work, friendly but all business. She breathed deeply to calm herself and unconsciously touched the locket.

"Hi, Amy!" Tom called out as he waved to get her attention. As he reached her, they embraced lightly and he kissed her on the cheek.

"I'm sorry I'm late. The doctor was running behind," she said.

"It's cool. I thought I was going to be late. I walked the entire length of the High Line, and I can't wait to show it to you. It's awesome," Tom enthused as he steered Amy, his hand on the small of her back, toward the side door of the restaurant. Heading for the graffiti-framed door, Tom stared at a statue of the Virgin Mary in the window along with a sun-faded and cracked menu, both protected behind a thick single pane of chicken-wire-embedded glass. When lowered, a metal roll-down shutter painted a dark brown to match the lower half of the building protected the carved eight-panel wooden door from the graffiti artists. He opened the door for Amy and followed her in. The cool darkness of the interior enveloped them.

A smiling woman with streaked blond hair, older than Amy, approached from behind the cluttered bar. "Bonjour. Deux?"

"Bonjour," Amy responded and nodded.

"S'il vous plait, me suivre," the hostess said as she directed them toward the front barroom on their left. The room was half full and noisy.

"Le pardon; avez-vous une table dans um tout à fait coin?" Amy asked.

"Oui, cette façon," the hostess responded, smiling, turning, and leading them to a table for two near a window in the back dining room.

"Est-ceci satisfaisant?" she asked, holding out the chair for Amy.

"Parfait," Amy responded, taking the seat.

"My name is Miriam, and I'll be your server today. May I bring you tap, flat, or sparkling water?"

"Tap water," Tom responded, "and two glasses of Chablis."

"No wine for me," Amy interjected. "I'll have tea, please."

"Hot or iced?" Miriam asked, turning to look at Amy.

"Iced, please."

"Sugar or sweeteners?"

"None, thank you."

Walking over to the wall, Miriam picked up a blackboard, a chalk menu in a mixture of French and English. Returning to Tom and Amy's table, she placed the menu on the floor, leaning it against the back of a chair at the next table.

"I'll be right back with your drinks."

Tom placed his phone on the table.

"Please turn that off and put it up," Amy asked. "Can't we have a pleasant lunch with talk instead of tweets, texts, or emails?"

"Okay," Tom said, turning off the phone and putting it in his shirt pocket. Tom and Amy turned their attention to the menu and Tom asked, "How come no wine with lunch?"

"I don't want any. Um, I've—got a busy schedule this afternoon," Amy stammered. The hostess returned with their drinks, a small basket of bread, and a plate of butter. "Any questions?"

"I'll have the ham omelet, please," Amy said, smiling at Miriam.

"I'll have the goat cheese puff pastry," Tom said, reaching for a slice of baguette and his knife.

"Excellent choices," Miriam said, turning from the table.

"Why this place?" Tom asked.

"It reminds me of the café we ran into when we got caught in the rain in Paris, the day we went to the Museé du Luxembourg," Amy said. "You know, the one on Bis

Servandoni between Rue Férou and Rue Garanciére, in the sixth arrondissement."

"If you say so," Tom said, looking around. La Luncheonette was reminiscent of the many neighborhood cafés they had enjoyed in Paris five weeks ago: dark walls with a lot of wood, a slight down-on-its-luck look, utilitarian tables with white butcher paper over a white tablecloth, and plain, dark wood and brown leather-backed chairs, worn with use, probably the same ones placed in the restaurant when it opened in 1988. Pepper mills and glass sugar jars served as centerpieces. Cheap, stamped-metal knives and forks on white napkins and upside-down glasses waited for patrons. The primary window light left dark corners untouched, adding to the less-than-successful appearance. A few photographs, framed prints, wine advertisements, and a large horizontal mirror in a gilded frame, most of them canted to either side from time and gravity, were the wall decorations. A red Coca-Cola clock on the back wall seemed totally out of place, its face tilted to the right. The masculine, polished wood bar held excess glasses, serving pitchers, extra sugar jars, and a tray of tableware. There was no sitting or standing at the bar, and Amy could tell Tom didn't like its clutter.

Looking back at Amy, Tom said, "I see what you mean. How did you find it?"

"I came here a week ago with a group from the office. Remember, I told you I'm serving as senior advisor-associate on a team headed by that relatively new associate, Reggie Boykin? Well, as team leader, he thought it would be good for all of us to get together away from the office to discuss our strategy for obtaining the Oatley & Co. engagement."

"Oh, yeah, the distinguished Reginald Andrew Boykin IV. Why aren't you team leader? You're the senior associate at the firm and the partner-to-be in a few months," Tom said, buttering another slice of bread.

"Do you ever listen to me? A year ago, I told you about this guy, Reggie. He's older than any other associate. In his junior year of college, he dropped out and sold all his possessions except for his bicycle and a set of *The Great Books* he bought for a hundred and fifty bucks. He moved to Crozet, Virginia, rented a furnished one-room garage apartment, and did yard work to get by. He says he got up every day at 6:00 a.m., read for four hours, did yard work for four hours, and then either walked around town or rode his bike out to a trailhead for hiking. Eighteen months later he finished reading the books, re-enrolled in college, graduated, and entered NYU's law and MBA joint degree program. He graduated with honors."

"Why yard work?" Tom asked, reaching for another slice of bread. "That's kind of nothing, not like guiding fishing, kayaking, or hunting trips."

"He said his purpose was to read and reflect on what he read and how fragile life is. Yard work is physical, not mental. As he worked, he thought about what he read. When some special idea came to him, he'd jot it down on a pad he always carried with him."

"Hmm. What great life secret did he learn during this chill-out time?" Tom asked, tipping his wineglass to his lips.

"I asked him that, too. He says he doesn't want to ever take life for granted. He's too serious. Doesn't mingle well with other associates or share any thoughts or ideas. He never smiles and seems to be the unhappiest person I've ever known."

"Anyway, why come back to a place that reminds you of the last rain-drenched Paris afternoon?" Tom said, sitting back in his chair and smiling at Amy.

Amy, about to answer, saw the hostess approaching with their lunches. Miriam placed their plates in front of them. Amy looked at her omelet and realized it would feed both of them. Tom grinned as Miriam placed his goat cheese pastry on salad greens in front of him.

"May I bring you anything else?" Miriam asked.

"How about more bread?" Tom asked, holding up and wiggling the empty breadbasket.

"Certainly," Miriam said, taking the basket and turning away.

"This goat cheese is enough for both of us," Tom said, picking up his knife and fork. "Will you eat some?"

"No, but I'm giving you part of my omelet," Amy responded, cutting her ham and egg lunch in two and passing the larger piece over to Tom's plate.

Making room on his plate for the omelet, Tom replied, "Sure, I'll take half, but you need to take some of my goat cheese." Tom took a bite and a sip of wine. "Oh my God, this is amazing. Are you sure you don't want some?"

Miriam returned and placed another basket of bread on the table. "Merci," Amy said, smiling at her. Turning her attention back to Tom, Amy said, "No, thank you."

"Okay, why does this place remind you of that Paris café? There were better cafés we enjoyed while over there."

"The bathroom," Amy said, blushing and smiling.

"The bathroom? I don't understand."

"You don't remember? We were dripping wet, went into the loo to dry off, and when I unbuttoned my blouse to take off my bra, you started drying my breast. You don't remember the corner table we thought was going to collapse?"

"Oh, yeah. Your concern was the rickety table, but I focused on the sex. Getting a quickie with a café full of Frenchies eating lunch outside the door was great," Tom said, grinning with satisfaction and saluting Amy with his wineglass.

Amy leaned forward, looking into Tom's eyes. "It wasn't just a quickie for me. It was different, special. When you came inside me, it felt different, not an orgasm, something I can't explain. I've never felt a change like that before or since. The physical and emotional sensations were special. I don't know why, they just were. That's all I can say."

Tom leaned back in his chair, still grinning. "We always have good sex."

"It wasn't just sex," Amy retorted, sitting back in her chair and shaking her head from side to side. "Do you ever feel sex is as much emotional as physical?"

"Now I understand. I guess so—I don't know what you mean," Tom said, sitting up and taking another bite of his pastry and a sip of wine. "Sure you don't want some goat cheese? It's good."

"No, thank you," Amy said, picking at her omelet and looking across the room, lost in thought.

"Is it because of what I said last night?"

"What?"

"Is it because of what I said last night?"

"What did you say last night?"

"You know, when I teased you about getting a pooch."

"No," Amy said, rolling her eyes and looking away.

"I didn't mean it," Tom said.

Amy turned to look at Tom again. "That's interesting, because you said it, didn't you?" She put down her fork and pushed away her plate. "How's your new job going?"

"It's fine. The training is over. I'm assigned to the dividend department."

"Do you like it?"

"Financial operations suck. It helps pay my share of our rent. It's the same thing day after day. Nothing cool like being a park ranger or guiding people on hunting or fishing trips."

"Tom, what do you want to be doing five or ten years from now? Do you think about that?" Amy leaned forward, looking intensely at him.

"Hell, no. I'll be thirty in a couple of months. There's too much living to do instead of worrying about five or ten years from now. I'll be doing something I'm passionate about, and making a lot of money doing it. What that'll be, I don't know. I'm interested in life now, not in trying to figure out how to be a suit in ten years," Tom said, shifting in his chair and reaching for his near-empty wineglass. He looked at his plate and then the breadbasket.

"What about a family? What if we want to have a baby?" Amy said hesitantly, looking down at her plate and reaching for her iced tea glass.

Tom's head jerked up, and he looked at Amy. "I don't want a baby! Jesus, are you crazy? We have a good life. There's plenty of time for strollers, dirty diapers, and no sleep. God, don't even talk about babies."

"Excuse me, Tom. I just asked. Babies happen, you know," Amy snapped, her eyes wide.

"That's why they have abortion clinics," Tom retorted, leaning forward, the two of them staring at each other.

"You—you could do that to our—your creation?" Amy said, sitting upright. Her eye rims and face turned crimson, and her chin quivered slightly before she caught herself and regained composure.

"Yes, of course," Tom said, sneering at Amy. She was taken aback by the cruelty on his face. She had seen that cruelty before when Tom thought he had the upper hand in a situation, but not intended for her.

"Damn, that's a tough decision," Amy said, looking out the window. For the first time she saw the small, wooden man doll sitting in a miniature chair on the windowsill next to a headless, armless, and legless naked female torso. An oversized clay pot holding a dying begonia sat on the other side of the torso, filling up the space. Amy thought it was a strange window combination for a restaurant as she digested the implications of Tom's vehement response.

"Not for me," Tom screeched.

Amy saw Tom as if for the first time. She meant nothing to him except a means of sexual release and a trophy to show off to his friends. Disgust, anger, and panic rose from deep inside her. She stared at him, making the situation clinical, all business, but realizing she was doomed and not wanting to give him the pleasure of knowing the predicament she was in.

Tom sat back in his seat and said, "Look, you're set in your career. Hell, this time next year you'll be a partner in your firm, rolling in dough. Anyway, when would you ever have the time to be a mother? Christ, you work seven days a week, don't get home most nights until almost eight. I'm for sure not going to be changing diapers, feeding a kid, and screwing up my life doing those things while you're having a good time. We get by pretty good. Ten years from now, I'll be doing something that makes the money you do. I just don't know what, nor do I care about that right now. We're in the sweet spot of life, so why talk about the unknown future? Babies aren't part of our life. Forget about that. I was thinking, I just walked the High Line. It's so cool. You haven't seen it yet. Let's go on the High Line Saturday morning. We'll take a picnic lunch and hang with people up there. There are so many cool places for two people to be alone or meet others."

"I know," Amy interjected.

"What do you mean, you know? We haven't been there."

"Reggie and I went up to the High Line after the lunch meeting."

"Oh? What did you and Reggie go up there for?" Tom scooted forward in his chair.

"To discuss the strengths and weaknesses of the Oatley team and show me how the High Line is changing Chelsea and the Meatpacking District. What was the best part for you?"

"The graffiti is so cool, and so are the art installations and the places people can meet," Tom said after finishing his wine.

"Not just the graffiti and outsider art," Amy responded, "but also the demolition and new construction. The opportunities to finance these projects, as well as joint venturing and syndicating projects, are enormous. Reggie set up a spreadsheet detailing property ownership on each side of the High Line from the Hudson River to Seventh Avenue. He's already contacting owners, soliciting their business, and coming up with ideas to work together."

"Well, do you want to picnic Saturday?" Tom snapped at her.

"I can't in the morning. Reggie has called a team meeting that will last until four," Amy said. "We could go afterwards, bring some small bites and a bottle of wine and watch the sunset."

"That's okay. Maybe another time. I'm hanging with Billy and Scott in the afternoon. We're kayaking the Hudson."

Miriam seated a man and a woman, both in navy pinstriped suits, at the table next to Amy and Tom. Amy noticed they both carried leather briefcases, his scuffed and worn, hers new and smooth. Miriam turned the menu so the new couple could read it and took their drink orders. She left and returned balancing three cassoulets in her hands for three construction workers in grimy T-shirts, dirty jeans, and dust-covered brogans at a nearby table. The workers' hard hats sat on the floor under each chair. She refilled the workers' water glasses and walked over to Amy and Tom. Picking up their plates, she asked, "Did you save room for dessert?"

"No, thank you," Tom and Amy answered in unison.

"Est-ce que ce sera séparée ou ensamble?" Miriam asked, looking at Amy.

"Séparée," Amy responded, reaching for her Ricky bag.

Chapter Two

Amy sat at a small, round table in an uncomfortable metal chair on the High Line. She didn't comprehend much about her surroundings, even the way the chair caused her legs to tingle. Nor could she read through her tears the huge sign on the corner of the self-storage building across the empty space between the High Line and the building. It said something about apartment space being smaller than something else. She was trying her best to stifle the sobbing noise that involuntarily came up from her chest. She thought about how unladylike and unprofessional she was acting. Milliseconds after she chastised herself, the severity of her situation and the devastating choices she had to make caused her chest to tighten and her heart to skip a beat again. Intermingled with the choices was a realization she must start implementing one or more of those choices now, today, without the luxury of sitting there on the High Line crying like some teenager. Her mascara and makeup ran down her cheeks and dripped on her suit jacket and skirt. She knew she would be appalled at her appearance if she could see herself.

Her right hand held a wad of tissues, while her left hand was tightly closed in a fist, with her red fingernails digging into the palm. The fist was pressing into her thigh. Her anger burned as intensely as her devastation at the decisions she would be forced to make in the next twenty-four hours. She was angry with Tom, but that anger was slight compared to the fury and contempt she had for herself. Amy knew Tom was history. She knew there was no going back to the way it had been. She'd thought the Paris trip would bring them closer together, but it hadn't. Reflecting on her predicament, she realized she had known before Paris that her relationship with Tom was not going to be long term. Why, then? Why go? Why continue to share his bed? Why had she allowed herself to be on the edge of hell with no choice to survive?

She was angry with her grandmother, who had drummed into her head from the first time Amy got her period till her granny died, "Don't have sex with anyone you don't want to spend your life with." Easier said than done. What are the signs, the clues? If she could sit on Granny's lap again, the answers would be whispered in her ear. But she couldn't. That's why Amy was angry with herself. She knew the signs. She saw them. But like so many others, she ignored them in the emotions and good times of the moment. Now, she had to make a choice: abort this innocent child growing inside her or lose the career she had worked so hard to develop. It had taken six years of long hours, hard work, some luck, and blind dedication to her firm to reach the point of becoming a senior associate and soon a partner in one of the most prestigious financial engineering firms in the country—no, the world. As sophisticated as the partners professed to be, she knew they would never make an unwed pregnant woman a partner. The physical condition spoke of carelessness, particularly in this age of easy contraception. The question of who the father was and why she was unwilling to marry him spoke volumes about her decision-making. There was only a slim chance she would be kept on as an associate. If she was, she was confident it would be with the understanding that she would resign shortly after the baby was born.

Panic sent a tremor through her body. Did she have the courage or callousness to abort a child because of a career? Did she have the courage or senselessness to throw away a career to raise a baby as a single parent? How did single parents raise a child in New York City? Could she afford to live in the city while working a job that allowed her time to care for the child? Would she be forced to leave New York, go somewhere else, and settle for third- or fourth-class work in her field? How could her life come to an abrupt halt just because she hadn't paid attention to her grandmother?

She was still crying but not sobbing when she heard a voice say, "There you are! I've been looking up and down the High Line for you."

Amy tried to dry her face, turning away from Reggie's voice.

"My God, are you alright? Amy, what's the matter? What can I do to help?" He pulled the chair from the other side of the table and sat at her side.

"I'm fine. How did you find me, and why are you looking for me?" Amy muttered.

"I'm sorry to disturb you, but I didn't want to go to a partner with this question."

Amy took a deep breath, dried her eyes, and said, "What question?"

"Chris Oatley called. He was all businesslike and said Merchant Capital had called him and proposed working on his project at half of what our fee is. He wanted to know our response to their proposal."

"That's typical Chris. I've been his contact at our firm for years and have given him good advice on small issues without charging him, building a relationship. I know for a fact he's used that free advice to grow and improve his business. He wants the best advice he can get for as cheap as he can get it. Go back to him and tell him we are confident our guidance and advice are worth the fee we charge. If he doesn't agree, we wish him well in his relationship with Merchant Capital, and we appreciate any future opportunity to work with him."

"You want me to tell him to go elsewhere?"

"Reggie, our fees are highly competitive and our work for clients is top notch. Chris knows that. You can't blame him for asking, but you must be confident in what we do and what we charge. Yes, if he walks, no one will blame you. The partners take pride in what we do and how competitive we are."

"Okay, I'll call him. Are you coming back to the office?"

"No, not today, and I may be out tomorrow. I'll let Margaret know later."

"Anything I can do?"

"Not unless you know how I can find a furnished apartment in the next thirty minutes."

"That's easy." Reggie pulled out his phone. "I'm texting you a local outfit that does short-term rentals in the city. I guarantee you they will have you in one in an hour if not thirty minutes."

"You're kidding."

"No. Next problem?"

"You can't help with that. If this apartment situation works out, I'll owe you one."

"Alright, I won't pry. See you in the morning. Thanks for the advice. It fits, if you know what I mean. That's what I thought should be the answer, but I didn't have the confidence to tell him that. I guess we're even," he said as he stood up. It did not go without notice that Amy couldn't look at him and she never smiled.

As soon as Reggie was gone, Amy called Lyft and arranged to be picked up at the foot of the Eighteenth Street stairs. She called the apartment company while walking to the stairs and arranged a furnished studio for two weeks. On her way to her soon-to-be former residence, she went by the rental firm, paid for the two weeks, and picked up a key. The time stress was greatly relieved, but she felt nauseated every time she thought of the decision she had to make by tomorrow.

In the car, Amy took her apartment key off her key ring and put the new, shiny key on. A short time later, she sat in her soon-to-be former apartment at the table in the open-plan living room. Her left hand clasped the locket around her neck. She looked around the living room, seeing the nondescript couch with the NY Giants lap blanket as a cover, the three straight-backed chairs that doubled as dining chairs when company came over, and the overstuffed recliner that Tom used as his base of operations when watching the sixty-five-inch flat-screen TV mounted on the wall. The tables in front of the sofa and alongside the single recliner were thrift store finds, while the dining table where she sat had been found on the sidewalk on West Twenty-Eighth Street. The posters and prints on the walls were of the outdoors and sports. She had moved in with Tom over a year ago, and not a single piece of the furniture or artwork was hers. Tom had picked out the bedroom suite—a queen bed, two nightstands, and dresser, the $899 President's Day Special package bought right after she arrived—even though she paid for it. She had two drawers in the dresser, with most of her clothes on hangers in the closet or in boxes on the two shelves she'd had the building super install for her. On the bright side, she was thankful it was so easy to erase her presence from the apartment and the relationship. She yearned for her grandmother's wise counsel! Turning her attention to the task at hand, Amy wrote Tom a note.

> *Tom, today's lunch finally opened my mind to the fact we are in different worlds when it comes to what we want now and for the future. I've come to understand this. Paris was my hope to recapture the magic of the past. It failed. You are a great guy, but not the right guy for me. Nor am I the right person for you. I've moved out. I'm leaving later this evening on a business trip to Chicago. I will be back Sunday afternoon. If you wish to talk, call my cell Sunday after one o'clock. We had a good time together. As it has been said, let's remember fondly the good times and not dwell on the fact our relationship is over. I wish you well in your future. Amy.*

Amy realized she had no tears for her relationship with Tom. She held her locket in her left hand and thought about how strange that was, given how much fun they'd had these past fifteen months. She thought of what needed to be done this week and felt the fear of the unknown well up inside. Her eyes began to burn. Could she do it? Would she be aborting a daughter or son? Would he or she have been creative, smart, athletic, and the type of person she wanted to be? Her thoughts turned quickly to the list of tasks necessary to get through the week. She ordered a Lyft car, left the key on the note, and started taking her bags down to the lobby.

After arriving at the studio apartment, Amy plopped down on her new sofa and looked out the window to west Manhattan. Between two buildings she could see a sliver of the Hudson River. She felt good in this apartment. It would be the right place for her to recuperate from her procedure and build the rationalization she would need to live with the decision. First, she had to change clothes and take her suit to a cleaner, stock up on food for at least three days, and buy what she needed to make this new place a home for at least two weeks, maybe longer. When she returned from shopping, she would make the appointment for tomorrow or Wednesday at the latest.

Chapter Three

Tuesday morning, Reggie sat at his desk and looked at his computer screen. He had googled the last name of the doctor Margaret said Amy went to yesterday. There were two doctors with the same last name. One was a plastic surgeon on Park Avenue and the other was an ob-gyn on Thirty-Third between Seventh and Eighth Avenues. He realized a beautiful young woman in her late twenties did not have any use for a plastic surgeon unless she had a skin cancer to be removed. Even then, hysterics were not called for unless it was melanoma, but if it was skin cancer, would Amy have been so secretive? There's no shame in getting cancer. A beautiful young woman in her late twenties, not married, could get hysterical over being pregnant or having a serious STD. Reggie felt a chill as he realized the ob-gyn was likely the doctor Amy had seen. It somewhat fit with her leaving her boyfriend at the same time. Perhaps he'd told her to have an abortion. Perhaps she'd realized she didn't want to marry him.

Reggie thought about the ramifications of Amy being pregnant and single at the firm. He knew she wouldn't be selected for a partnership. That would not happen at this firm. Would they allow her to stay as a senior associate? Maybe. Doubtful. What will happen to me if Amy gets the boot? he wondered.

His job should be secure, particularly if he brought the Oatley account on, but he would no longer have a mentor. Amy had been spot-on yesterday with her advice about handling Chris Oatley. The phone call had gone smoothly, and the papers were now in Oatley's inbox for his signature. Our team meeting Saturday, he mused, will solidify everyone's assignments in onboarding this new client and structuring recommendations for the future. Will Amy be there? He hoped so. She had said she may be here today, so he could ask her and tell her of their success.

Reggie saw Amy go into her office and close the door. The tradition at their firm was an open-door policy. If a door was closed, the person did not want to be disturbed. Reggie felt she wouldn't mind if the interruption was for good news. He went over, knocked lightly, and opened the door.

Amy looked irritated. "Don't you know by now what a closed door means?" she snapped.

"Yeah, but I thought you would want to know that, as we speak, Chris Oatley is signing the engagement papers. Your advice about him was spot on. Saturday's team meet will distribute assignments for the onboarding and recommendations. Will you be attending?"

"That's all good. Congratulations. I don't know if I can make the Saturday conference, but I'll try. Thanks for the tip on the apartment. It worked beautifully. Now, if you'll excuse me, I've got calls to make and reports to write." She turned her attention to her computer screen.

"Yeah, sure. Glad it worked out. Perhaps later we can talk." Reggie left her office. The rest of his day was inundated with prep work for the Oatley account. Three partners came by and congratulated him on successfully capturing the engagement. Shortly before five, Reggie went back to Amy's office and saw that she was gone. He walked over to their shared assistant's desk and asked, "Margaret, has Amy left for the day?"

"Yes."

"Would you leave her a message? I need to speak to her early tomorrow morning when she arrives."

"She's not coming in tomorrow, nor Thursday and Friday. If you need to communicate with her, I suggest you shoot her an email."

"Is she on assignment? I didn't hear of any new projects."

"All I know is she has a doctor's appointment early in the morning, and she said she would be at home and I could get her on her cell or by email."

"Thanks. I'll email her."

Reggie knew the implications of what Margaret had said. Amy was going to have an abortion or surgery for a female issue. He bet it was an abortion. She didn't understand the ramifications of the procedure for her now and later in life. His hands started twitching. He crossed his arms and put his hands under them. What could he do? He realized her welfare at the firm was critical to him, but her attitude this morning had shut him out. Thoughts of Jenny flashed into his mind. Sweet Jenny, forced to choose between a real bad decision and a horrible decision. He googled the doctor's address and put it in his phone.

Chapter Four

The early morning chill was still prevalent, even as summer was obviously on the way. The sun was just coming up as Reggie leaned against the wall by the entrance to the doctor's office. He didn't know how long he'd have to stand there, just that he had to try to give Amy a third option. He knew he must be at the top of his salesman's game today, and even that might not work. He had to try. She deserved a third option. He continued to read the *Wall Street Journal* as a Lyft car pulled to the curb shortly before seven. Amy got out and headed to the door with her head down.

Reggie folded the paper and said, "Amy." Startled, she looked up at him. Her eyes were bloodshot, her face flushed from crying, and she had on no makeup, even lipstick. Reggie thought she was beautiful.

"What are you doing here?" she snarled. She tried to push past him, but he enveloped her in his arms. "Get your arms off me."

"Amy, please. I just want ten minutes of your time. Ten minutes to save you a lifetime of regret and possibly guilt. I promise I will leave and never speak of this situation in the future. Please. Ten minutes."

"I don't know what you want, or think is going on, but ten minutes."

"Let's go across to the bagel shop. Ten minutes, that's all."

Reggie bought both a bagel and coffee. Amy ignored her coffee and didn't touch the bagel. She said, "Okay, Reggie, ten minutes. What's so important it couldn't wait?"

"You are. I believe you're pregnant and going into that doctor's office to have an abortion. I believe you're doing that because it's the least bad choice since you will lose out on your partnership and possibly your job if you're a pregnant single woman. I believe you are taking what you think is the best way out of this dilemma.

"There is a third option. Marry me, today. Everyone at the office knows we have worked closely together for the last four months. Jokes have been made about the beautiful young associate and the pretty boy. I've heard them, and I'm sure you have. Here's my proposition to you. We get married and let it be known we have had a serious relationship since before you went to Paris. You move into my apartment. I've got two bedrooms; you'll have your own bedroom with a lock on the door. There won't be any sex. We'll be a loving couple in public. At the apartment, we'll share expenses and duties such as cooking and cleaning. A couple of months after the baby is born, we'll get an amicable divorce, and you'll have your own life back, your partnership, and your baby. A short ten-month charade keeps you from making a horrible mistake that is irreversible, keeps you on a partner track at the firm, and allows you the time to decide if you want to keep the baby or put it up for adoption. That's it. Did I mention no sex?" Reggie sat back in his chair.

Amy looked at him, tears still streaming down her face, her right hand at her breastbone, enveloping her gold locket.

"I've got to go; my appointment is at seven and they said not to be late." She rose from the table and walked out the door.

Reggie rose and followed her. She rushed across the street, but the traffic caught him and when he finally made it across, she was entering the doctor's office. Reggie felt good that he had tried. It was a long shot, and he knew it. They had never flirted with each other. She must think he was nuts or some sort of pervert who couldn't have a normal relationship with a woman. He opened his newspaper and began reading section two. Women went into the doctor's office at a steady pace. They looked at Reggie with some suspicion, which made him move from the building's front to a tree out close to the street. Leaning against the tree, he felt a knot boring into his shoulder. He didn't know how much time it took to have an abortion and recover, but he was determined she wouldn't come out of the office without seeing a friendly face, even if she didn't want one. She couldn't be alone, even if she thought she wanted to be. It was just too dangerous. He shifted to his other shoulder. Shortly after seven fifteen, the doctor's office door opened, and Amy tentatively walked out. She stared at Reggie, a frown on her face.

"Look," he said, "what you just did will physically be over in a few days. Your psychological healing will take much longer, if you ever heal. I just want to be of assistance, any way I can, and be a friend you can talk to without any repercussions. No one will ever know from me." He smiled and held out his hand to her.

"No sex?" she stammered, at the same time reaching up to touch her locket.

"No sex."

"I pay half the rent, half the utilities, half the food, do half the chores, and have first dibs on the bathroom in the morning."

"There are two bathrooms, you can have the primary bedroom with the bathroom en suite. I'll take the other bedroom and the hall bathroom."

"No, you keep your room. I'll take the other one. Finally, you agree we will get an amicable divorce two months after the baby is born."

"All correct. You didn't have the abort—procedure?"

Amy started crying and shaking her head no. Reggie dropped the newspaper and wrapped his arms around her. He whispered, "You did the right thing. Every day going forward, you will know that." He closed his eyes and silently thanked Jenny for her help. "Let's call a car and go to City Hall so you can become Mrs. Reginald Andrew Boykin IV."

"No. If I'm going to be married, I want to look decent and, oh God, respectable."

"I understand. I want to look my best as well."

"What time is it?"

"Seven twenty-five."

"I'll meet you at City Hall at ten thirty."

"You don't want to share a car?"

"No," Amy whimpered. "I still can't believe I'm doing this." She looked back at the doctor's office door. Reggie took her hand. It was limp and ice cold. He felt she was second-guessing her decision.

"Why don't we share a car? The driver can drop you off first, take me to my place, and go back and wait for you."

"No! Look, what you're doing is noble, and—" Amy looked around, searching for the right word. Finally, she looked back at Reggie. "—stupid. I don't understand your game. We'll take separate cars. Both of us need to let your scheme sink in."

"Amy, it's only for ten months. Then you're a partner, we get a divorce, and you have your position at the firm and a baby. You can choose to keep the child or put it up for adoption."

Tears started flowing again. "Oh God, is this really happening? How dumb am I? Please call a car before I change my mind."

Amy stood in the bright sunshine in a navy blue suit, a white blouse with pleats down the front, and black pumps, her ever-present Ricky bag over her shoulder. She nervously toyed with her gold locket on a delicate gold chain as she half-smiled at Reggie, who wore a pinstriped black suit, a white shirt with French cuffs, and lion head cufflinks with emerald eyes. His gleaming black boots complemented the silver-and-black striped tie. The coolness of the morning had given way to the rising heat of the day. Reggie reached for Amy's hand and took it, but she pulled it away and reached into her Ricky bag. "Here is a hurried draft of our agreement. You should look it over before signing to make sure you agree to the terms."

"Do you have a pen in that gorgeous pocketbook you always carry?"

"Of course. You going to read the document now, right here?" She handed him her Montblanc ballpoint pen.

"Turn around and I'll use your back to sign on." She did so and felt the pressure of his signature flourish on her back. It sent chills through her body. She turned back around to face him.

"Now you turn around, and I'll sign," she said. "You really should have read the agreement first. You don't know what I may have stuck in there." He turned, she signed, and he returned to looking at her.

"There is one other paragraph you need to add to the agreement. If you are going to be The Fourth's wife, you need to have rings that reflect that fact. I have my grandmother's rings. She wore them for the seventy years she and my grandfather were married and the two years after he died. She left them to me for my bride. When we get our divorce, I'd like them back. Do you agree?"

"Of course. Can't we just go buy some simple rings?"

"Not if we want people to believe we're serious about our marriage. I want you to wear these rings; I just want them back when you're ready to move on."

"What about a ring for you?"

"I'm going to wear my grandfather's ring." Reggie reached into his jacket's inside pocket and pulled out a small velvet pouch. He shook out the three rings. Putting his grandmother's engagement and wedding rings on Amy's left-hand fourth finger, he looked at her and said, "They fit! That's unreal."

Amy looked at the platinum and diamond rings. The engagement ring, a single European-cut diamond surrounded by rectangle diamonds, and the wedding band of small, round diamonds were stunning. "Reggie, I don't know what to say. These are gorgeous. I see why you want them back. I'll add the paragraph and give you a copy of the agreement. I can't wear these; they're too valuable. How big is that stone?" She held out her hand and looked at the rings.

"The center stone is five carats, and the rectangle diamonds add up to another two carats. The wedding band totals two carats. They look magnificent on your hand. Come on, soon-to-be Mrs. The Fourth. Let's go get hitched." He took her hand, and they went up the stairs. Amy noticed Reggie never smiled.

♥

"Ｔｈａｔ ｗｅｎｔ ｗｅｌｌ, ｄｏｎ'ｔ ｙｏｕ think?" Reggie plopped down on the sofa, untying his tie and unbuttoning his collar. "Harry's face when we told him said everything about the surprise, even though there was gossip about us. I don't know about you, but his arranging the reception in thirty minutes spoke volumes about his regard for his senior associate."

"It was just as much for you as for me. Reggie, what are we going to do about our families? My parents believe in the 'bird method' of parenting."

"What's that?"

"You know, raise them until they can fly on their own, then push them out of the nest. There's only one exception to that rule. My mother is going to go ape over not being able to plan a big wedding and invite her friends. They all try to one-up each other. Dad, however, will be delighted at not having to pay for a big wedding. I imagine he'll buy himself a new BMW." Amy sat in an upholstered chair positioned as part of a group around a table in front of the sofa. Spaced around the room's walls were small oil paintings, some representational, some portraits, and some abstract. Even covering the broad spectrum of art, it was clear the same educated eye had selected each one. There wasn't much furniture, but except for the sofa and upholstered chairs, the pieces looked to be fine wood and either antique or early twentieth century. They were eclectic but fit well together. Two custom-crafted bookcases with glass doors dominated the wall opposite the sitting group. These were the only new pieces in the room. In the bookcases were new, old, and very old books. She made a mental note to examine his taste in books. While she had never collected books up to now, she was an avid reader. She wondered what the bedrooms looked like but didn't want to ask. She knew she would see them soon enough. Her thoughts were more about the absurdity of their situation, and, increasingly, the realization of her vulnerability. Amy felt all alone. She didn't even have a close girlfriend whom she could confide in and get feedback and moral support from. The cost of being blindly ambitious toward her career hit home for her.

"Yes, Mother will be sad she can't get a couture dress and waltz down the aisle as the mother of the groom. I bet your dad will be delighted he doesn't have to pay for a huge ceremony. You think about it tonight, and we'll do whatever you want tomorrow. My suggestion is the two of us call our families on FaceTime and tell them together so they can see the two of us and how happy we are. That way, each family can see the new spouse appears to be an upstanding citizen. I'm sure the mothers will decide to have big welcoming parties in the future. Our job is to get them to postpone the events till next year so we can get divorced first and spare them the expense."

"You're right, but I think each of us had better speak to our parents alone first so they don't have a heart attack or say something crass with the shock," Amy said, reaching up and touching her locket.

"May I ask you a personal question?"

"That all depends. How personal?"

"I notice you seem to touch your locket often. What is the significance of it?" Amy opened the locket and held it away from her so Reggie could see inside. On the left was a picture of an elderly woman with a broad smile and a few strands of brownish-gray hair curled around the photo. The right side was empty.

"This is my Granny. Before she passed away seven years ago, she was—no, she still is—my rock. She gave me unconditional love. Even when I messed up, she let me know she loved me but was disappointed in my actions. I wouldn't be the person I am without her boosting my spirit, her guidance in all areas, and her belief I could be whatever I wanted to be. I've never loved anyone like I loved her, and, frankly, don't believe I ever will." Amy closed the locket. "My Granny's grandmother had given it to her when she turned thirteen. It was her most prized possession. She gave it to me when I went off to college, so, as she said, 'You can always have me close by to give you comfort.' She said I should leave the other side empty until I found someone I could love unconditionally, who loved me the same way."

"That's quite a story. Thanks for telling me about her. I understand that kind of love." Amy noticed Reggie looked away from her before he asked, "Are you staying here tonight?"

"Really? I'm glad you do. No. All my clothes are at my temporary apartment. I've paid two weeks' rent. I haven't thought much about it, but it seems to me it would be best if I stayed there until Sunday and then moved in here."

"You coming back to work tomorrow? I know you told Margaret you were taking the rest of the week off."

"I did, but that was when I thought I would need recouping time. I think it best to get back to work. I'm almost behind in some analyses."

"Which projects?"

"Culpepper Industrial's potential acquisition of Watson Millworks. Have you done any analysis on the project?"

"No, I haven't been exposed to it."

"Culpepper wants to absorb Watson in an all-stock merger. Culpepper shareholders will end up with 72 percent of the combined firm. Watson's price is a little high. Using Watson's price and some synergies in the merger, it will still take at least three years to be accretive to earnings. Since we're representing Culpepper, I'm putting together some pro forma statements, breaking down assets to see duplication, looking for improved R&D outcomes based on what each firm is now doing, and looking for a lower price that makes the deal work for Culpepper but doesn't cause Watson to walk away."

"Sounds interesting. Want another pair of eyes to look at it? I've had some experience in that type of analysis."

"Yeah, but I must get Jerry to agree to your signing the confidential memo to see the numbers. That shouldn't be a problem. I'll do that first thing in the morning. Now, I'd better be on my way. Crazy. Unreal crazy."

"What's crazy?"

"Sleeping alone in a studio apartment on my wedding night. Not what I thought it would be like." Amy looked at Reggie and tried to smile but failed.

"I'll walk you back to your place, if you want."

"Thanks, but no thanks. This has been a different kind of day. Amy Leonard leaves in the morning to get an abortion and ends up Mrs. Reginald Andrew Boykin IV, married to a stranger by noon. I've got to have alone time to process it all. Why, Reggie? Why screw up your life, even for ten months?"

"I'm not exactly a stranger; we've seen each other every day for two years. We've worked closely on the Oatley engagement for the past four months. I guess I understand, but I don't feel like a stranger. I'll do my best not to crowd you, Amy, but I think we need to have some code word that will give me a heads-up to back off if I try to smother you. We do, however, need to give the appearance at work and with friends of a loving newlywed couple. What code word do you want to use?"

"The word *divorce* will do. I understand." Amy took off the engagement and wedding rings. "Keep these here. I don't know how smart it is to wear such beautiful and expensive rings on the streets of New York. When we're going someplace where it's appropriate, I'll wear them. I'll go tomorrow and get a simple gold band to wear on a regular basis." She looked at Reggie and saw the disappointment in his face. "Reggie, please don't misunderstand me. I would die if something happened to those rings. I'd also be most unhappy if someone cut off my finger to get to them. I want to wear them every day, but that doesn't make sense in these times. When we go out with friends and for special occasions at the office, I'll be proud and happy to wear them. Does that make sense?"

"Yeah, I guess so," Reggie said with a frown. "Do you want to meet me here in the morning, or should I come to your place? If we're newlyweds, it won't make sense to get to the office at different times."

"Hmmm . . . I'll come here so I can bring some of my stuff each morning. That way, all Sunday won't be wasted moving. Maybe we could go to Central Park and enjoy the outdoors."

"Great." Amy noticed Reggie's spirits brightened. She pulled out her phone and called for a Lyft car.

♥

AMY SAT ON HER SOFA, staring out the window at the sliver of the Hudson River that was visible. Her pulse boomed in her ears as her blood pressure rose while she twirled her cell around and around between the thumb and index finger of her right hand and held onto her locket with her left hand. She thought about all the reasons to not make this call, but she owed it to Reggie to tell her parents about their marriage. Even though they practiced "bird parenting," they were still her parents, the grandparents of this baby growing inside of her, and now Reggie's in-laws. God, how she wished she could call her granny first. She hit the FaceTime button on the phone and silently hoped they would be out as it rang. On the fourth ring, her father answered.

"Hi, Daddy. It's Amy."

"What, you think I'd forgotten your lovely face and name? How's my big-city, high-powered financier daughter?"

"I'm fine, Daddy. Is Mom at home? I want to talk to the two of you."

"Yeah, she's here. Hold on." Amy heard her father yell for her mother. A minute later, her mother's face crowded in next to her father's.

"What's the matter, Amy?" her mother asked immediately.

"Nothing's the matter. I just wanted to tell the two of you some good and surprising news. I got married today." Amy held her breath.

"No! You're kidding, right?" Amy's father said.

"I knew your promiscuous ways would get you knocked up someday. Do you know who the father is? Is it that same kid you roped into living with you?"

"Agnes, for Christ's sake." Amy's dad turned back to the camera. "She didn't mean that crap, Amy. I'm sure congratulations are in order. Tell us about your new husband."

Any's voice faltered, then she composed herself. "His name is Reginald Boykin, and he works with me at Global Advisory."

"What happened to that fella you were living with, Tom what's-his-name?" Agnes asked.

"We broke up, Mom."

"Will we get a chance to meet your new husband soon?" Amy's father asked.

"Yes, at some point. We want to have a Zoom call with you tomorrow evening. Our schedules are such we won't be able to come down until March."

"March next year?" Her father asked.

"Yeah, Daddy. That's not so long. We can Zoom on a regular basis in the meantime. Is eight tomorrow night a good time for me to introduce y'all to Reggie?"

"Make it seven. Your father and I never miss the Hallmark movie that comes on at eight," Agnes said.

"Mom, please be nice tomorrow evening. Reggie is a wonderful guy, and you'll like him. He means the world to me. I don't know what my life would be like without him. You'll like him. He's a real gentleman in all respects."

"Amy, don't worry. Your mother and I will welcome him with open arms, won't we, Agnes?"

"Of course. I'm just happy it's not one of the string of losers you've dated."

"Alright guys, seven tomorrow evening. Daddy, I'll text you the Zoom instructions. Love y'all."

Amy clicked off and let her emotions go. She brushed the first tears away but let the rest just trickle down her face. She wondered if her mother would make snide remarks to Reggie and reached up to touch the locket. Granny had always countered Agnes's nasty, degrading remarks to Amy with uplifting and positive praise. Amy knew life would be different without Granny soothing the cuts from her mother's tongue-lashing. Amy could never understand her mother—being high school valedictorian and getting a full scholarship to Georgia Tech, an invitation to join Phi Beta Kappa, and a full scholarship to the John Hopkins MBA program couldn't please her. Why? Amy couldn't understand them. Never could she confide in either parent. They just didn't seem to want to know. She took deep breaths, consciously controlling her breathing, calming down. She knew she had to make the next ten months work, not just for herself, but for a really good guy. She felt so bad for Reggie, but this charade was his choice. He said it was to save his career. That was a flimsy excuse for taking on a pregnant woman, particularly when there was no sex involved. She knew she had to get some sleep. She must play her part to the hilt. She owed him that. Fleetingly, she wondered if Tom had read her note yet.

♥

REGGIE SAT ON THE SOFA amid doubts about what he had done. Amy's apparent resistance to closing the emotional distance between them was disappointing. He didn't expect her to cheerfully embrace the plan, but he did expect her to at least engage at some level. The basic question kept coming to his thoughts, why had he proposed the third option? Ten months, about half of the time he'd spent in Crozet, wasn't all that long. If Amy made partner, his job would be secure, and he would be on a partner track with her in the inner circle. For that, ten months was not too long. He knew she didn't love him. She might not even like him. Did that really matter? Two people who don't like each other and are thrown together argue. He didn't think that fit in this case. She might not like him, but she would be on board because this whole deal was done to save her. What exactly did he think of her? He knew she was beautiful, brilliant, and a caring person. He didn't believe he had strong feelings for Amy, but he liked her.

Amy had said the scheme was stupid. Maybe it was. He just knew he had to do it. If he hadn't, he didn't know whether he could continue trying to get better. He understood. Closing his eyes, he made a promise to make the situation work. He knew it was a step in his healing process. He accepted the risk that if their deception was discovered by the firm, both he and Amy would lose their positions. Did he think the risk was worth it? Yeah, because he could already feel the aching emptiness within him shrink a little.

Chapter Six

Amy lay in bed wondering how life could change so dramatically in an instant. *Black swan event* was the term they used for unexpected disruptive actions influencing her business, but she'd never thought about black swans in her personal life. Thinking about it now, she realized that the sudden death of a family member or friend was a black swan event. The demise of her relationship with Tom had to be a sort of black swan, or perhaps a gray swan. She had hoped Tom would be ecstatic about having a baby with her. She saw the irony of knowing Tom would have made a terrible marriage partner but wanting him to love her enough to have a child together. How could she have been so wrong? She remembered that she had told Tom she was available Sunday afternoon to talk. What would she do if he called when she and Reggie were at the park? How would she tell Tom she was married to Reggie? Maybe he wouldn't call.

Amy fixed coffee and heated an English muffin with a thin slice of ham and one scrambled egg. Looking around the studio apartment, she knew she was going to make the bed and close the sleeper sofa every morning. She shuddered at the thought that even for a few days the apartment would look a mess if she didn't put everything together each morning. She wondered if Reggie ate breakfast. She wondered what time he got up in the mornings. She realized he probably didn't get up at five like she did, or do the stretching exercises, or have breakfast while reading the *Wall Street Journal* on his iPad. She smiled to herself, thinking he was about to have his routine changed.

Amy and her suitcase arrived at Reggie's building at six thirty. She went in and told the desk attendant she was going to 7C, the Boykin apartment. He called and Reggie told him to send her up. Again, she realized that The Fourth's world was different from Tom's world and a step above what she was used to. To her surprise, Reggie was dressed and ready to go.

"Let me have that," he said, taking her suitcase. "I'll show you to your room." Amy followed him through the short hall to a reasonably sized bedroom with a queen bed, two night-stands with lamps, and a chest of drawers. One straight-backed chair was in the corner. Spartan, but obviously high-quality furnishing. "Your bathroom has a place built in as a dressing and makeup space. Come, I'll show it to you. Don't expect much because this is an old building, and I've chosen not to upgrade any of the bathrooms or the kitchen." Matching white towels and washcloths with a white shower curtain gave the older fixtures a certain amount of class.

"Thank you," Amy said. "We've never talked about our time at work. I usually arrive by seven and stay until seven each day during the workweek, and on Saturday I get in by nine and stay as long as necessary. Now, as a married woman, how does this schedule mesh with my spouse's?" she asked.

"My schedule has been close to the same. I'm good with yours. Perhaps we can alternate each day picking a restaurant for dinner if we're not going out for drinks with co-workers or friends. I'd also like to agree that unless one of us wants to go with a group of the same sex, we always go together."

"Makes sense until I'm as big as a house. Then you'll have to be on your own." Amy looked at him without smiling.

"When you're as big as a house, we'll come home together and I'll fix your dinner here." Reggie wasn't smiling, either.

"I'm sorry I called you a stranger last evening, but we don't know anything about each other. I don't know your favorite color, college, football team, sport, exercise program, or any of those little things people in love and married know about each other. Know what I mean?"

"I tell you what. We both have an intense schedule at the office today. Why don't we play one hundred questions tonight over takeout Chinese and a cold bottle of Perrier?"

Amy smiled and said, "You're on. You can have wine or alcohol if you want."

"I'm drinking what my wife is drinking," Reggie responded, unsmiling.

They left for the office.

Chapter Seven

Staring at the ceiling, Amy was wide awake. She didn't know if her inability to sleep was due to her new surroundings, which was strange since she'd had no problem falling asleep in her temporary apartment for the last five nights, or to the realization she was now fully engaged in a trumped-up marriage with the guy in the room on the other side of the wall. Their agreement was to keep up pretenses until the baby was two months old, which would be sometime in March. Is it possible to live with a stranger for that long? she chastised herself. Of course it is; think of him as a college roommate, no more than that. The only problem with that logic was she hadn't been pregnant in college and her roommate had been another woman, not some hunk that could be a poster on a teenage girl's bedroom wall. She turned on her side and felt her abdomen. Whatever she thought about the craziness of this situation, her insomnia likely came from the pending meeting with Reggie's parents, who, once they were told their son had eloped, said they would fly in next weekend to see the newlyweds. Neither Amy nor Reggie had expected that. She was relieved the call with her parents had gone off with only minimal nasty comments from her mother. They had promised to call regularly.

Amy knew Reggie had saved her from the two bad choices she had gotten herself into. Why had he done it? He said it was selfish. Her being a future partner was important to him, and he gave his associate position at the firm as the reason. But she didn't believe that fit with the way he was acting now. Although he still seemed unhappy in all aspects of his life, he seemed more mellow when it came to their arrangement even though it had been just a few days. A sensation ran through her body, causing her mind to go blank. She remembered Tom was likely to call Sunday afternoon. She and Reggie were supposed to go to Central Park to have a picnic and just get to know each other. What should she do? Leave her phone at home or turned off? Would that just postpone a confrontation that might later happen at work? The only thing Amy knew was she owed it to Reggie to tell him about Tom's call. She tossed and turned until early Sunday morning.

Normally she was not a shy person. When living with Tom, and before that, when staying overnight with a boyfriend, she'd just thrown on a man's shirt over her panties with no bra underneath. This first Sunday morning as Mrs. The Fourth, Amy felt she had to get completely dressed before seeing Reggie. She had heard him go out earlier and return. The aroma of coffee permeated the apartment. They hadn't talked about food. She thought they would have their first grocery shopping event when they were returning from the park. If necessary, she could go down to the corner bodega and pick up something. She took a deep breath and unlocked the bedroom door.

"Well, there you are, Miss Sunshine," Reggie said, getting up from the sofa. The *New York Times* and *Post* were scattered on the sofa table, floor, and end table. "How about some coffee? Do you like milk and sugar with your coffee?"

"Yes, please. Very little milk and two sugars. That's a comfortable bed. I can't believe I slept so hard," she lied. "It looks like you're an early riser." She nodded toward the papers.

"Yeah, the morning is my time. If I'm up early, I have time to read the papers, to think about what's going on in the world and how it may affect me and my position at the firm."

"The last three nights, getting to share what we like and don't like, was good. I feel more confident as your supposed wife. I didn't think—"

"Amy, you are not my supposed wife," Reggie interrupted. "You are my wife. It might only be for another ten or eleven months, and it might not be a conventional marriage, but it is a legally binding marriage."

"You're right. Please be patient with me. Growing up, I never pictured my first marriage, the only one I ever thought about, as an arrangement like this."

"Frankly, I never thought about marriage. I just figured when I was hit by a lightning bolt of love, it would happen. I always sort of left it to chance," Reggie responded, not looking at her.

"Lucky you."

"Ready for breakfast? We didn't cover meals last night, so I don't know if you like a big breakfast or a small one. When I got the papers, I picked up some croissants, butter, jelly, ham, and eggs. You interested?"

"Usually, I just have coffee, buttered toast, and one egg, but a croissant and butter would be great. You want some ham and eggs? I know how to scramble eggs and fry ham."

"No, I'm a light breakfast eater too. Why don't we save the ham for sandwiches I can make for our picnic today?"

"Okay." Amy looked around and saw the toaster oven in the corner of the kitchen counter. "You ready now, or do you want to finish reading the paper?"

"It's early yet, so let's read for a while. Let me reassemble the paper and you can pick your section."

"On the weekends, I usually start with the society section. Usually, I don't read the *Post*."

"That will save any arguments over the papers. I don't read the society section and love the sports in the *Post*."

Amy sipped her coffee, sitting at the dining table. She looked over at Reggie on the sofa, with the section of paper he was reading folded in a neat way. His face was serious with a frown. She realized the one-hundred-question quiz was not enough to reveal who he really was. Unconsciously, she reached up and fondled her locket. More importantly, she wondered why he had taken on this burden to save her from herself. She respected his intellect and professionalism as a financier and thought of him as an interesting guy, but she didn't love him. She was confident of that fact.

Both Friday evening joint calls to parents had gone well, except for Reggie's mother's hinting about Amy being pregnant causing the rush. His parents did not ask for the new couple to come see them. Instead, they were coming to see the newly-weds, would be staying at the Carlyle, and expected the four of them to have Friday night dinner and spend Saturday together before they flew home that evening.

Amy, putting down her section of the *Times*, realized now was as good as any to tell Reggie about Tom's pending call. "Reggie, there is a matter that I need to settle. Before your proposal Wednesday morning, I had left a note for Tom at his apartment. It told him I would be out of town until Sunday and if he wanted to talk, he could call me Sunday afternoon. He's likely to call today." She looked at Reggie to see his reaction.

"Do you want to take the call?" Reggie asked, a disappointed look on his face.

"I think I should. He needs to know we're married. I want to sever the relationship cleanly and quickly."

"Would you like to be alone when he calls or meet him somewhere?"

"No. I definitely don't want to see him, and as your wife, I don't ever want to have any call from a former boyfriend that you don't know about and hear, particularly from Tom."

Reggie's look of doubt turned into a frown. "I've got a similar situation. For the last four months I've been seeing a young woman. Her name is Isabella Devoneaux, and she's a junior partner at Evans, Wilson, and Crandall. We knew each other at NYU Law but didn't date until we met by accident in a used bookstore a few months ago. Both of our firms were working on the Marchman merger. I'll need to tell her tomorrow since we're scheduled to have dinner Friday night." Amy hid her surprise that Reggie had a girlfriend. Discovering this fact confused her even more. Why was he doing this?

Amy nodded. "Look, Reggie, if this woman means something to you, why don't you have dinner with her? I've put you in an awkward position and it's not fair. I'm a mess. You're a knight in shining armor. You shouldn't become a monk because of me. I'd feel better if you weren't so hobbled in your life by my intrusion."

"Amy, you're my wife. I'm married now. I was raised by parents who instilled in me that vows of any kind, particularly marriage vows, are to be kept. It's a matter of respect—respect for you, Isabella, and myself. I'll call Isabella and break the news to her over the phone. I don't want to lead her on, and I don't want to be thought of as a philanderer."

"I didn't mean to disrespect you. I feel terrible for the situation you're in." Amy fought back tears, took deep breaths, and turned away from Reggie. He got up and went to where she was sitting. He put his hands on her shoulders. At first, she tensed, then relaxed.

"Well, Mrs. The Fourth, as you call yourself, I don't see any reason these calls should ruin our picnic in the park." Amy was relieved at his casualness about her talking to the father of her unborn child, the one that he, Reggie, was pretending was his, and strangely she felt a slight pang of jealousy at knowing Reggie had a girlfriend.

Chapter Eight

The sun played peek-a-boo behind puffy white clouds that raced across the blue sky as Reggie and Amy strolled down Sixth Avenue, choosing it for the accessibility of bathrooms at Bryant Park. Tourists were everywhere. Bryant Park was starting to fill up with individuals at small tables reading the paper or conversing with others. Children ran around the green spaces, while the vendor kiosks selling drinks or food responded to the long lines of New Yorkers and tourists.

As they walked, Reggie would take hold of her elbow at every street crossing. Amy thought the movement cute. At Fiftieth Street the crowds on the curb were thicker and the traffic heavier. He took her hand as they walked across. At first she reacted with stiffness. On the other side, he did not let go. By the time they reached Fifty-First, she liked the idea of walking hand in hand. She forgot about the pending phone call and became lost in the beauty of the day, the picnic in the park, and the pleasure of having a guy, a good-looking one at that, care enough about her to hold her hand. She realized they hadn't spoken a word since leaving Bryant Park and that felt perfectly natural.

Strolling down Literary Walk on its cinder surface, surrounded by the foliage of the magnificent American elms, they decided on the footpath to the west of the Bethesda Fountain for their picnic. There was a steady stream of people walking by, headed over the iron bridge, as well as a good view of the crowd at the fountain where snake handlers, musicians, and bubble creators held court, looking for donations from the crowds. The fountain, the lake beyond, the shade tree overhanging the bench, and the steady breeze made it an ideal setting for an afternoon picnic in the park. They laid out a multicolored dish towel of Amy's between them on the bench. Reggie went down the hill to a food vendor and bought two Cokes. They ate and made small talk, getting to know each other. Time seemed to melt away until Amy's phone rang. They both tensed. She looked at the screen and saw it was Tom. She smiled weakly at Reggie, swiped the screen, and said hello.

"Amy, hi. This is Tom." He then hung up.

"He hung up," Amy said, looking at Reggie.

"That's strange. What did he say?"

"He said my name and identified himself. He'll probably call back. What were we talking about?"

"How you like to do laundry two times a week in the evening. You'll be glad to know, in that closet in the hall is a stackable washer and dryer unit. It's not used that much, but it does the job." He raised his eyebrows. "Do we need to draw straws for who gets to use it on what night?"

"No, we can flip a coin. Heads, you do both our laundry. Tails, I watch you do the laundry." Amy giggled as it took Reggie a few seconds to catch on. Then she heard a shout that startled her.

"Amy! Amy!" She turned and saw Tom coming up the walkway.

She looked back at Reggie. "I'm sorry."

Tom reached her as she stood.

"Tom, what are you doing here?"

"I wanted to see you, not just talk to you."

"How did you know I'd be here?"

"My phone app. It tells me where the person I'm talking to is located." He tried to hug her, but she pushed him away. He was startled, then saw the food on the bench and looked at Reggie. "Who's he?" Tom asked.

"Didn't you get my note?"

"Yeah, but who is he?" Tom pointed to Reggie.

"That's my husband, Reggie Boykin."

"What the—! Did you say your husband? You can't be serious. You never even liked him."

"We were married Wednesday."

"No, that can't be. The note said you were out of town on business. You can't do this to me. What will our friends say? This isn't real." Tom paced from side to side, alternating running his hands through his hair and tightly hugging himself. "Do you have any idea what you've done? You're my girl, not his. I've set up for us to go meet the crowd this evening at O'Reilly's. I'm going to look like a fool."

"Tom, I told you in the note that we were through. Didn't you read it?"

"Yeah, but I didn't believe it. Married? Oh my God, what will people think of me?"

"Tom, tell them you broke up with me. They're your friends, really. Make up whatever story you want. If by chance I see one of them and they say something, I'll tell them you broke up with me."

Tom's face flushed; his arm shot out with his finger pointing at Reggie. "Why him, pig? Why Reginald Boykin? You gold-digging for the money, pig?" Tom's face was bright red and his forehead was wet with sweat. Reggie moved from his relaxed position for the first time.

Then Amy spoke in a calm and controlled voice and demeanor. "Because I love him. I've loved him since I got to know him in February. I just wasn't sure. That's why you and I had our trip to Paris. I wanted to be sure. I am sure. Tom, you and I are on different wavelengths about what we want. That doesn't make either of us wrong. It just means we're not meant for each other. You'll come to understand that in time. You're a good person, just not right for me." She was as surprised as Tom and Reggie at what she said. She hadn't planned it. The words had come out, not tumbling in a fury like Tom's, but clinically calm, giving them a deeper meaning and finality. She knew they hurt Tom, but avoiding hurting him wasn't nearly as important as burying her relationship with him in the past. She thought about the baby growing inside of her. That baby was more important than Tom's feelings. She thought about the guy sitting on the bench who was willing to screw up his life with a pretend marriage to save her baby's future life and her own professional and psychological well-being.

The sting of the words, and the way she calmly said them, took the fight out of Tom. His arms fell to his sides. "Well, I guess I'm lucky. Yeah, I'm glad I got rid of you since you're a two-timing whore."

"Don't call my wife names," Reggie said as he stood and squared off in front of Tom. "You had over a year to show her how much you loved her, and you blew it. When you look in the mirror each morning, know you're looking at the reason she's gone from your life." Tom stared at Reggie, who was a couple of inches taller and more athletic looking.

"This isn't over, whore. You'll pay for cheating on me," Tom snarled as he turned and walked away.

Amy sank to the bench and used her napkin to wipe away the tears.

"Don't cry, Amy. He's not worth the tears or emotions," Reggie said as he stroked her hair gently.

"I'm not crying for Tom. I'm embarrassed you had to see that ugly scene. I'm so sorry I got you into this situation," she sobbed as people walking by stared at what they thought was a lovers' quarrel. "I think we should go home."

"Sure, let me clean up the bench." Reggie began carting the remainder of their picnic to the trash container. He finished his Coke before discarding the can. Returning to Amy, he touched her on the shoulder and said, "You ready?"

She nodded and stood up, then drew herself up to full height and surveyed the park. "Such a beautiful place for such an ugly scene. I had no idea he had an app that would tell him where I was." She turned to Reggie and said in a low voice, "I am truly so sorry I got you into this mess."

He pulled her to him and hugged her, putting his lips close to her ear, and said, "You didn't get me into a mess. It was my idea for us to get married, remember? For the next ten to eleven months, we're in this together."

She shuddered, pulled away, looked at him, and said, "You're the strangest guy I've ever met, but thank you. Let's go home."

"We will, but first we need to go by Verizon and get new cell phones with numbers Tom doesn't know." They started walking. Amy tentatively took Reggie's hand. He looked at her and securely wrapped his hand around hers.

♥

REGGIE DIDN'T KNOW IF HE should be angry or concerned. He was quiet as they walked. As they came to Fifth Avenue, he took a deep breath, stopped, turned to her and said, "You really don't like me?" Disappointment was evident on his face.

"I didn't say that to Tom. The only times we talked about you were when you joined the firm and over our lunch last Monday. I didn't say I didn't like you. I said you were the most unhappy person I've ever met. Tom was just striking out to hurt us. Please understand, we barely knew each other until this week when we had our questioning sessions."

"I'm trying to get used to this situation as well. The light just changed, so let's get to Verizon." Reggie decided to accept the reality that Amy was in this situation because she wanted to save her baby and her career. Next his thoughts turned to Tom. He was confident Tom would be and could be the flaw that brought the whole situation crashing down. He needed help with what to do. He did know that Joseph, his best friend and former college roommate, could help him, but he wondered how much to tell him. If he revealed everything, would Joseph think he was nuts? Would he think less of Amy, ensuring there would not be a close relationship between the two couples? Allowing his analytical mind to create a decision tree, he finally settled on telling Joseph that Amy had a boyfriend she broke up with when she and Reggie fell in love. The boyfriend had threatened Amy in a confrontation. The question was simple: how do we get Amy's ex to leave us alone?

Chapter Nine

Monday morning, as they walked to the office, holding hands, Reggie said, "Amy, I'm going to call Isabella this morning at ten. I feel calling her at the office will give me an excuse of another call coming in if my conversation with her goes badly. Will you come to my office to sit in on the call?"

"No. Our circumstances are different. In ten months, I'll be a single mother without any interest in a social relationship with a man. You'll be able to renew your social life after our divorce with your head held high as a real stand-up guy. You need to find a way to maintain a friendship with Isabella for the future. I'll say it again: if you wish to see her discreetly during the next ten months, I'll understand. Discreet is the operative word, not for my sake, but because no one should think you're anything other than an honorable and first-class guy." Reggie kept a firm but gentle hold on Amy's hand.

He sat with his back to his desk, his head laid back on his chair, and his eyes closed. His door was closed and the blinds on his glass wall were drawn. He thought about Isabella and the first time they had met. He had gone to The Strand used bookstore one Sunday just to browse. He wasn't looking for anything in particular, just a book to fill one of the many subject holes he had in his growing library. He noticed her first. She was dressed in blue jeans and an oversized sweatshirt. Nevertheless, she was stunning with her naturally blond hair, pale complexion, and bright red lipstick. When she looked up from the book she was skimming, he smiled, and she smiled back. Thirty minutes later they were sitting at an outside table talking books and law. Their conversation lasted for hours. The relationship blossomed from there. He knew she was never going to be his wife, but he thought they made an interesting couple with two circles of friends that mixed well. He was actually glad Amy had chosen not to be in the room. He knew that Issie cared for him, even if Amy didn't. He thought about how ridiculous the situation was. Breaking up with a woman who showed her feelings of connection to be married to an emotionally distant one would probably make a psychology textbook somewhere. Why? He thought he heard Jenny say, "You know why." Finally, he realized he had to pick up the phone and call her.

"This is Isabella, may I help you?"

"Issie, this is Reggie. Do you have a few minutes?"

"Personal or business?"

"Personal."

"Hold on. Let me close my door." A few seconds later she said, "Alright, handsome, talk dirty to me."

"That would be nice, but I'm calling to break our dinner date for Friday."

"Okay, is there something wrong? Did I do something to upset you?"

"Issie, last Wednesday I got married." Reggie stopped to let that comment sink in. There was silence on the line. "Issie, are you there?"

"Don't call me that. What do you mean, you got married? To who? Who did you marry? Were you sleeping with both of us at the same time? I can't believe this. Didn't we enjoy each other's company? I don't understand. Oh my God, what a way to begin a week—getting dumped by the guy you thought you had a future with. No! No! No! This can't be happening! Why her and not me, Reggie?"

"Issie—"

"Don't call me that, I said!"

"Isabella, it wasn't a choice of you or her. She just stole my heart. I don't know how else to say it."

"Who is she? Where does she work? What is her background?"

"Amy is her name. She is the senior associate at my firm. We've been working together on a major project since February. She's from Georgia."

"Do you love her?"

"Yes."

"Three weeks ago, we went to Hudson for the weekend. You can't tell me you weren't happy with us as a couple. I find this hard to accept. I want to see you. Meet me for lunch at Shorty's."

"Issie, er Isabella, I can't do that. I'm married now. I've taken vows of fidelity. That's important to me. I don't want to hurt you, but we can't meet." As soon as he said the words, the line went dead. Reggie replaced the phone in its cradle and sat back. His thoughts turned to Jenny and the situation he'd created for himself, partly on an emotional whim and partly to save the position of his mentor. He mentally thanked

Jenny that Amy wasn't in the room. In a soft voice he began talking to Jenny and explaining to both of them why he'd done what he did. He knew Amy didn't love him. That hurt, but he understood. He had mixed feeling about her. He just knew he had to give her a third option. "You understand that, don't you, Jenny?" he whispered. In the silence, he thought he heard her say yes.

Next, he called Joseph and explained the situation to him. Joseph proposed a simple restraining order, but Reggie thought that was too public. Besides, he doubted that Tom's threat in the park warranted it. Finally, Reggie said to Joseph, "Here's the real challenge. My wife is pregnant. Yes, that's why we went to the courthouse and got married."

"Does her former boyfriend know this?"

"I don't think so."

"What will he think when he does find out?"

"I don't know, but he seems to me to be a nasty kind of person who likes to make trouble if he feels he's been shafted."

"Okay, get me his full name, address, Social Security number if you can, and where he works. Let me put someone on it, and I'll get back to you."

"Joseph, I'll owe you a big one."

"You betcha. I'll hold you to it. When am I going to meet your new wife?"

"Soon. We're swamped with closing deals, but in a few weeks. How are Karen and the kids?"

"All's well. I asked her if she wanted another, and she said yes, in thirty years when these two are grown."

"I look forward to when the four of us can get together."

"I'll be back in touch, Reggie. Send me that info."

Reggie thanked God for Joseph. He got up and opened the blinds and his door. Before going back to his desk, he decided to get a donut in the break room.

Chapter Ten

Notwithstanding Reggie's phone call to Isabella, Amy and Reggie's work life turned into a routine. They were in their respective offices by seven in the morning. Except for interaction on the Oatley account and requests from Reggie for advice on other issues he was involved with, their contact was minimal. Lunch was usually a sandwich at their desks, rarely together. At seven in the evening, when everyone was gone, the first one finished went to the other's office. Rather than continue working, as both had done before the marriage, they were delighted to find a stopping place and leave the office without a briefcase full of files. They took turns deciding where they would eat and whether to go to a restaurant or take food home. Nothing was mentioned about the altercation with Tom, Reggie's phone call to Isabella, or the pending meeting with Reggie's parents. In Amy's mind, all three events swirled like a tornado, with Amy being swept up in it and finding Reggie gone, and she was all alone. Her anxiety shot up like a rocket, but she hid it from him by being emotionally distant. Finally, on Thursday evening, Amy raised the subject.

"What should I know about your parents, Reggie?" She gently moved the locket on its delicate gold chain from the right to left and back again, over and over.

"Just that they're happy people. My father, his father, and his grandfather have owned a bank for over eighty years. It's a community bank, always has been and always will be. He runs it conservatively. As he says, he's running it for his great-great-grandchildren. The family's well-being springs from the bank. There are other investments, of course, and these are important, also made with a long-term perspective, just like the bank. Mother sits on the family's business boards and is a housewife. She's the chairwoman of the university's medical school board and volunteers in the community. Before she and my father married, she was a nurse, practicing in the local hospital. That's how they met forty-seven years ago. Father and his buddies were quail hunting and he stepped in a hole and sprained his ankle. Since they didn't know if it was broken, his buds took him to the emergency room, where Mother was on duty. One thing led to another, and they were married a year later. It took them awhile, but I finally came along." Reggie diverted his eyes from Amy, and she noticed the movement.

"Just you? They didn't have any more children?"

"Mother had a difficult delivery. After that she couldn't have any more children. I'm the only one alive."

"Oh God, she's not going to like me. I've denied her a big wedding for her only child."

"Mother's not that way. She's different. She looks at life as reality, not as she wants it to be. She taught us, I mean me, to have the same perspective. It's an important one for being successful. See what is and make the best of what there is. Pretty simple."

"You call them Mother and Father. Are they so formal all the time? Are you going to tell them I'm pregnant?"

"Amy, you have to understand. My family has worked hard to be successful for four generations. During my great grandparents' time, when children came along, the nannies taught them that their parents should be called Mother and Father. It may seem stiff to most people, but within our family it's an endearment that doesn't seem formal. As to the pregnancy, I'm not going to deny it if it comes up, but, no, I'm not going to volunteer the information. That can come later. Let's stick to our story. We work for the same firm. When we were thrust together, we fell in love, and last week decided we wanted to get married. End of story."

"I'll do my best to make them like me."

"Be yourself, Amy, and they'll love you. I haven't seen them in two years, so there will be a lot of distractions to take the heat off you."

"Are we going to meet them at La Guardia or Kennedy?"

"Neither. They fly private, so they're coming into Teterboro. They have a car service bringing them to the city. We're going to meet them at the Carlyle Gallery at seven. Dinner is at Daniel's at eight thirty, so it will be a long evening. I'm not sure what Mother has planned for Saturday, but I know they must leave for Teterboro at four. It will be a fun time."

Amy smiled and said a short prayer to herself.

♥

REGGIE WORE HIS BEST PINSTRIPED suit with a silver tie and polished boots. Amy wore a maroon suit with a white silk shirt, her choker-length black pearls, and matching earrings with the locket hanging below the pearls. Reggie's grandmother's rings were on her left hand, and her Ricky bag was over her left shoulder. They were holding hands as they walked up to his parents' table. Both of his parents stood. Reggie gave his mother a bear hug with a big grin on his face. He then shook hands with his father and gave him a bear hug as well. Amy stood back, nervously opening and closing her hands. Reggie turned to her and said, "Mother and Father, may I present my beautiful wife Amy."

Amy stepped forward, holding out her hand to Reggie's mother, and said, "Mrs. Boykin, so nice to meet you."

"Amy, my dear, please call me Helen. Well, one thing is for sure, my son does know beauty when he sees it." She shook Amy's hand. Amy then turned to Reggie's father and held out her hand.

"I don't shake hands with my beautiful daughters-in-law; I hug them." He reached over and pulled Amy to him. Amy smiled and realized where Reggie got his propensity for hugging.

"Just one," Reggie said. "There won't be another, for sure."

"Great, he scared me there for a minute," Helen said. The four of them laughed. The evening was a laugh-a-thon, like they had known each other for years and weren't meeting their new daughter-in-law for the first time. Later, at their apartment, Reggie was all excited and Amy was relieved.

"You were a hit, just as I knew you would be. What an evening. Great wine, great food, and exceptional company. It couldn't have gone any better."

"What are you and your father going to do tomorrow? I can't believe your mother said she and I were going shopping, having lunch, and getting a mani-pedi at the Red Door." She looked at her fingernails. "I knew I needed a mani, but I didn't think it was noticeable."

"I assume you realize she just wants to put you under a microscope and see what you're really made of. You okay with that?"

"Helen is wonderful. Your parents are so easy to talk with and get to know. I'm looking forward to spending time with her. Now, I suggest we get some sleep. What do you think about going in Sunday to get Saturday's work done before Monday?"

"Great idea."

♥

"Helen, I've always felt it's better to have a few items that are high quality than a closet full of second-class fashion fads." Amy and Helen were having lunch at DB Bistro Moderne. They had the back right corner table in the main dining room, offering a full view of the restaurant. As is the nature of a corner, they sat close with Helen on Amy's right. The morning had consisted of getting a mani-pedi and shopping at Saks. After lunch they were going to hop in a car and finish the day at Carolina Herrera's a few blocks from the Carlyle. The morning had been enjoyable for Amy. Her only negative thoughts were how she wished she and Reggie weren't deceiving these two nice people. Amy had just taken a bite of her halibut when Helen spoke.

"How far along are you?"

Amy almost choked. "I'm sorry, what did you say?"

"I asked how far along you are. I was a nurse for eight years before marrying Reggie's father and for fifteen years after that, until Reggie came along. I can spot the glow and beauty of a young mother-to-be from across the room."

"Five or six weeks," Amy said in a low, trembling voice.

"Does Reggie know?"

"Yes."

"That explains the rush to a city hall marriage." Helen put down her fork and took a sip of her white wine. "Amy, I'm not one to judge when people who love each other, or think they love each other, consummate those feelings. All I know in this case is you're a lovely young lady and, more importantly, you make my son happy. I haven't seen the jolly-natured young man I raised since . . . well, for a long time. You've given me a great gift in knowing he is back to being the happy person I want him to be. Now, tell me, do you plan to find out the gender before birth?"

"I . . . we don't know yet. We've kind of thought it would be nice to be surprised when the baby is born."

"It's none of my business, but for what it's worth, I like the concept of not knowing until the delivery day. Some people will say 'the happy day,' but you, going through the agony of birth, will think the next day is the happy day." Helen put her hand over Amy's and squeezed it. "If you're willing, let's swap emails and keep in touch directly. You know, girl stuff about pregnancy, raising children, and training a husband."

"You're on," Amy said, relieved.

♥

"Reggie, I feel dirty deceiving your parents. Did your mother say anything to you about my being pregnant?"

"What? No, she didn't."

"Well, she picked up on it when we walked into the gallery. We were in the middle of lunch at DB's when she casually asked me how far along I was. I almost choked, but I told her the truth. You know what? She wasn't even fazed by the fact that I'm five or six weeks along and we only got married last week. Her total focus was on the fact that you were the, as she said, 'jolly-natured young man I raised.' Until last night I don't think I've seen you smile, much less be jolly-natured. Why have you been hiding your true personality?"

"I've not been hiding anything, just intensely focused on my career," Reggie said with a frown.

Amy sighed. "I won't pry. You were just a different person this weekend. Your parents deserve better than this arrangement. Your mother even swapped emails with me so we can share girl stuff about pregnancy, babies, and training a husband. Perhaps you should ask your father about training."

"No need to. All he'd tell me is to say 'Yes, dear. Whatever you want.' Amy, I hope a different and better person? Look at the situation like I do. What if neither of us could have children? We would adopt. Or if your husband, the father of your child, had died, I would adopt the child, and my parents would be ecstatic and treat the child as their grandchild. That's just the way they are. We're not deceiving them. If there is any deception, it will be the divorce we're going to get in ten months."

Amy started tearing up.

"Hey, no tears. It's been a fun-filled, successful weekend. My parents love you. You were everything they could wish for in a daughter-in-law. I don't know about you, but I'm ready to hit the sack. Sunday at the office will be a full day."

"I'll see you in the morning. I want to write your parents a thank-you note for their graciousness this weekend."

In the middle of the night, Amy suddenly jolted awake at the sound of someone crying and saying, "Jenny, why? Jenny, no! Jenny, Jenny." She didn't know where it was coming from, and it stopped almost as soon as she awoke. A few minutes later, she heard Reggie in the kitchen. She wondered who Jenny was. Could she ask Reggie if he was the one crying and talking? Was he talking in his sleep or awake? Could she help him? Should she ask him? She decided it was a former girlfriend who jilted him and none of her business. She wanted to help him but realized that since their arrangement was temporary, she should give him space. The weekend had gone better than she had ever hoped it would. She closed her eyes and returned to a restful night after a pleasant weekend as Mrs. The Fourth.

Chapter Eleven

Reggie, Amy, and the Oatley team returned from a lunch celebrating Reggie's thirty-second birthday. They carried a small cake, paper plates, and plastic forks into his office. As they crowded around his desk, they all saw a beautifully wrapped present. Everyone called for Reggie to open it. Not knowing where it had come from, Reggie looked at Amy and raised his eyebrows. She shook her head. He ripped off the paper and stood holding a two-volume set of *Ellwood's Sacred History*, the Old Testament volume printed in 1705 and the New Testament volume printed in 1709. Everyone knew their rarity and the corresponding cost. A card between the volumes fell to the desk. It read: "Found these while thinking about you. Love, Isabella." Reggie quickly turned it over. All the associates got a slice of cake and returned to their offices. Amy picked up the card and said, "Looks like you still have an admirer."

"Amy, I had no idea. I haven't spoken to her since my phone call weeks ago."

"Obviously she didn't get the message. Perhaps you should call her and see her discreetly."

"Amy," Reggie snapped, "you might not think much of our marriage, but I do. I've told you, I don't see women other than my wife. I'll have the books sent back to her today."

"Reggie, please don't be angry with me. I don't want you to suffer because of our situation. I do respect you and our marriage. I want you to understand that." She gave a half-smile, picked up her cake, and went back to her office. Sitting in her office, savoring a bite of the cake, Amy thought about Reggie. Isabella had shown she was determined to have a relationship with Reggie. How would Amy feel if he changed his mind and did want to see her? How would she feel? He was different from the guy she had worked with before the marriage. Still, Amy noticed a deep sorrow she couldn't seem to alleviate. She made it her mission to help him overcome whatever was bothering him during the remaining months of their marriage. She owed him that and more for giving her a third option in her dilemma.

At seven, they left together holding hands. These walks to and from the office were like winding up springs in the morning and releasing the tension in the evenings. They shared information about the transactions they were working on, getting and giving advice. When it was raining, they zigzagged with their umbrellas from one building with scaffolding to another. Even when there was no rain and they left home before seven and stayed until seven at night, they still sought out the scaffolding to enjoy the coolness on hot summer days. They always held hands, even when one or the other was demonstrative with their free hand or holding an umbrella. They discussed what they would do for dinner or what fun they would have on the weekend. Knowing that Amy would increasingly become less mobile, in the early weeks they hiked in Hudson River Park or took Citi Bikes to Central Park and walked in the park or in the Met. Everything suggested the arrangement just might work.

♥

TOWARD THE END OF THE week, Amy had a morning appoint-ment at a client's office uptown. When finished, she thought she and Reggie could have a light dinner of chicken salad, grapes, asparagus, and flatbread. She had the Lyft car meet her at Eighty-Fifth and Madison. While waiting to pay, Amy saw Julie Wilson, a former friend of hers and Tom's, more Tom's than hers. She turned, hoping Julie wouldn't see her.

"Amy, long time no see. You look great," Julie said, looking Amy over, recognizing her in the check-out line at Dean & Deluca on Eighty-Fifth. "What are you doing up this way?"

"Hey, Julie. I had a client meeting at their office, and I thought I'd get some D&D chicken salad and grapes for dinner tonight."

"I'm so sorry to hear about you and Tom. Y'all made such a cute couple. It must have been terrible the way he dumped you. He's such a stinker. I'm so sorry."

"It was terrible, but you know, as they say, life goes on," Amy lied but was secretly happy Tom had told everyone he dumped her. She forced a smile, hoping that hump in her ten-month charade marriage was cleared.

"Yeah, he didn't miss a beat taking up with that Emily Reddick."

"Who?"

"Tim Reddick's sister. She's pretty but a real naive country girl. She moved here a couple of months ago. She's staying with Tim until she finds some roommates to share an apartment with."

"Good for them. I hope they're happy."

"Yeah, but what I don't understand is the prick is telling everyone that you're pregnant, he's the father, and he told you to get an abortion." Julie looked Amy up and down again. "You don't look pregnant." Amy's heart skipped a beat and she coughed. She was thankful the Eisenhower cut of her suit jacket hid the abdominal bulge that was beginning to show. "What pissed me and some of the other girls off was he said you were careless about your birth control, and that was your problem, not his. What a douchebag he can be." Amy shifted the chicken salad containers so her gold wedding band didn't show and rolled her eyes in mock disgust.

"Julie, it's good to see you. I've got to run. I've got a car waiting to take me back to my office." Amy didn't give Julie time to respond before she turned and escaped into the safety of the car.

Riding back downtown, she felt dread over what was obviously a problem brewing with Tom. Holding her locket, she smirked. That was just like the sleaze he was to find himself another bed partner but continue to badmouth the last one. He had done it when they hooked up, so why was she surprised that he was doing it now? She couldn't understand why he would tell people she was pregnant and that he'd dumped her because she wouldn't get an abortion. She switched to her financial analyst mindset and then understood that he was so self-centered, he couldn't see that people looked at him as less than a man for abandoning his pregnant girlfriend and supposedly their child. She knew she had to tell Reggie. It worried her that their careful charade was coming apart. If it did, she didn't know what the ramifications would be, but she dreaded them.

<h1 style="text-align:center">Chapter Twelve</h1>

Reggie had gone to get a *Sunday Times* and *New York Post* while Amy was getting dressed. She came out and, finding Reggie gone, went over to the bookcases. Opening one door, she picked a volume at random and looked at it. It was *Scott's Last Expedition,* Volume 1, printed in 1913. At that moment the apartment door opened and Reggie came in.

"Do you like books?" he asked.

"I'm an avid reader, but it's generally work-related nonfiction and romance novels," Amy said, giggling.

Putting the papers on the sofa table, Reggie went over to the bookcases, opened all the doors, and said, "You're welcome to read anything that strikes your fancy. This is the beginning of what I hope will be a comprehensive library one day, in a huge double-height room with a library table in the middle, a ladder for reaching the higher books, two comfortable chairs for reading, subdued lighting, and the aroma of old and dusty books. Collecting books is my passion, but I don't do it the way most bibliophiles do. I do like the first edition, but not for what most collectors want first editions for; I want them because they're usually the purest thoughts the writer had, before the public or publishers were able to interject salability or censorship into the process. Most book collectors are more worried about the condition of the dust jacket than the words in the book. I'm not. If you promise not to laugh, I'll show you just how obsessed I am."

"I promise," Amy said, impressed by Reggie's earnestness. He reached down to the bottom shelf and pulled out a five-by-eight-inch green-covered Moleskine book. He opened it and handed it to Amy. In his precise handwriting was a list of subjects, some with numbers next to them.

"This is my goal—to have books from as many time periods as possible on each of the subjects you see listed. See the number?" He pointed to the page Amy was reading. "Every time I buy a book, I record the subject matter by adding to the Category's number. That way, when I go on one of my hunts, I take this book with me, pick a topic, and search for a book. Inevitably I also find something else. That's when the pleasure goes off the scale."

"I'd like to go with you sometimes. I don't know what to look for, but I can learn," Amy said, smiling. "That is, if you don't think I'll be in your way."

"I'd love for you to join me. Hey, we have no plans for today. Let's go this afternoon. Two of my favorite stores are within walking distance. We can put on our grubby clothes and root around in the dusty shelves. It's an exciting time. At least it is for me."

♥

"Reggie, look what I've found. This is a set of letters from the Marchioness de Sévigné that she wrote to her daughter, the

Countess de Grignan, in 1668 to 1688, with these volumes published in 1801. They must be some interesting letters to be considered important enough to be published over 113 years later."

"Great find! Let's add them to our collection." Reggie turned one of the books over and over in his hands, lost in the excitement. Amy realized she had not been this excited about shopping in her entire life. She realized he didn't really mean it, but it felt good that he'd said *our* collection. She wondered if he'd ever said that to Isabella. Momentarily she felt she was truly married, until the specter of their agreed-upon divorce intruded on her happiness. Book hunts became special and sensual times Amy looked forward to. She wondered if the hunts would be as magical after the divorce, without Reggie.

Chapter Thirteen

The first week of August, a FedEx envelope arrived for Amy at her office. She opened it without looking at the address. Inside was another envelope with her name written in a beautiful script. She opened it and found a note and a check for five thousand dollars. The note read, "Amy, please use the enclosed for your mommy clothes. Best wishes and thank you, Helen." Amy's face flushed and her eyes burned. She fanned herself with the note and check. Walking to Reggie's office, she handed them to him. He read the note, looked at the check, whistled, looked up, and said, "Can I come shopping with you, or do you want it to be a girlie trip?"

"Do you really want to do that? It could be boring."

"Not getting to see you modeling clothes. Yes, I'd love to come if you don't mind."

"I don't mind. Let's do it Sunday."

"You're on." Amy returned to her office and sent Helen a thank-you email, letting her know that Reggie was going shopping with her and they would send videos of the excursion Sunday night. She signed the email, "Love, Amy." Before hitting send, she thought about the word *love*. She didn't know if it was too forward, but she hit send before overthinking it. Her feelings for Helen's kindness were real, even if more than her feelings for Reggie.

♥

"I GOT SOME GREAT VIDEO to send to Mother about what you bought," Reggie enthused as they left Saks. Turning left on Fifth Avenue to walk back to their apartment, they were confronted by Tom.

"You're pregnant. I knew it. How far along are you? That's why you quizzed me about babies at our last lunch. I bet you're having my baby. You should have told me instead of running off and trapping another guy in a marriage." Tom turned to face Reggie and said, "You weren't the only one humping her, so there's as much a chance that mistake she's carrying is mine."

Reggie took a step forward, but Amy grabbed his arm. "Tom," Reggie said, shaking off Amy's grip and stepping between her and Tom, "are you saying that Amy's baby is yours?"

"Yeah, that's exactly what I'm saying," Tom said, trying to see Amy.

"Well, I hope you're right. You'll hear from my attorney by Tuesday, so you'd better get an attorney to represent you. We're going to settle this parental issue once and for all. Now, please leave us alone, or I'll call the authorities." Reggie took Amy by the hand. They turned and crossed Fifth Avenue, headed to Sixth Avenue.

When they got to Sixth and Amy couldn't see Tom behind them, she stopped and turned Reggie by grabbing his arm. "What did you mean, 'I hope you're right'? Reggie, please explain what you meant."

"Amy, this is no place to discuss this. As soon as we get home, I'll explain everything. Look at me, Amy." Reggie put up his hand to turn her chin away from Fifth, where she was still looking to see if Tom was following them. "Amy, look at me. Have I done anything that would give you doubt about my wanting to protect you and your happiness? You must trust me until we get home."

At the apartment, Amy didn't know whether to run into her room and cry or stay in the living room with Reggie. She clasped the locket and her chin quivered. How could she ever have felt this charade would work? She had thought people at the office would see through it, but she had been sure Tom would move on. He really didn't love her. He may have enjoyed her body, but that was it. She couldn't understand why he was so doggedly pursuing her.

Reggie spoke up and brought her back to reality. "Amy, what about a glass of Perrier while I explain?"

"Yes, please. No, how about three quarters of a glass of chardonnay? I haven't had alcohol since lunch with your mother. The baby won't mind," she said as she rubbed her bulging abdomen. "Why doesn't he leave us alone?" Tears started flowing. "Damn these emotions. Sometimes I can't help but cry. This is not like me." She slammed her fist on the arm of the sofa.

"It is like you, in two ways. First and foremost, you are a caring person carrying a baby. Second, your pregnancy is making you more emotional as you grow that baby inside of you."

"What are you now, a doctor?"

"No, but I've been reading about the subject now that I'm an expectant father."

"Reading about it?"

"Yeah," Reggie said, his face flushing. "They have all kinds of books for expectant dads."

Amy looked at him. His sincerity gave her pangs of guilt and sorrow. He was truly a good person. He was also unflappable, particularly as this road the two of them were on got more twisty and dangerously close to the edge of a crumbling cliff, potentially leaving them falling into an abyss. "What's with Tom? What are we going to do?"

"Tom is a serious concern for us and you in the long term. If he continues to go around telling everyone he's the father of your child, which he has been doing, it will begin to stick in people's minds, particularly if you don't refute the accusation. Eventually, the story will get to someone at the office. If you're confronted there, you can't tell a lie, or you'll risk both of us losing our jobs for deceiving the firm. We must stop Tom once and for all. My sophomore and junior years of college, my roommate was Joseph Harrington, now a junior partner at the Miller Wilson law firm. Have you heard of them?"

"Vaguely. What's their specialty?"

"Family law. The best in the country. Very expensive, but Joseph owes me."

"What do you mean, he owes you?"

"He would have never made it through English Lit our sophomore year if I hadn't spent hours getting eighteenth-century writings through his thick head. We've kept in touch through the years. He's one reason I went to Crozet instead of out west during my time away from school and the world. He was a big support. Really, my closest friend, like a brother. Anyway, I reached out to him right after our altercation with

Tom in the park. He thought about the situation and developed a plan to get Tom out of our lives. He's been waiting to see if Tom would cause any more problems. I'll call him in the morning and tell him to proceed."

"Why didn't you tell me you were concerned?"

"Amy, I'm not really *concerned*, just cautious."

"What's the plan?"

"He hasn't told me yet. He says there is some risk, but he's stacked the odds in our favor. He has built a file on Tom and feels confident in the outcome of the hearing. What I do know is we will all have to appear before a family law judge. Joseph said one of his partners can get a judge to hold the hearing in chambers so it won't be public. We must go through with it so we can avoid a messy situation later. Please, Amy, know your best interest is my primary focus."

Amy sipped her wine. "Do we have any crackers left from last night?"

"Sure." Reggie got up from the sofa and went to the kitchen. He came back with a small plate of Ritz and a container of tuna fish salad he had made for their dinner the night before.

Amy reached over, spread some tuna on a cracker, and said, "Want one?" She held the cracker out to Reggie.

"Yes, thank you." He took the offering.

Amy reached up and held her locket. "Reggie, I've got to trust you, but trust is kind of new to me. I've never been this vulnerable and felt this scared since my granny's death. The truth is" —the tears started flowing again as the words tumbled out in a torrent— "you're all I have and that petrifies me, not because you're a bad person—you're actually a wonderful and kind person—but because if you walk away from me, I'll fall to pieces." She finally had to gasp for breath. She sat there, looking and feeling like a little girl of five, all her aura of being the smartest, prettiest, and most in-control woman abandoned.

Reggie pulled her over to him, and they half sat and half lay on the sofa, her sobbing and him stroking her hair and whispering, "Get it out. Get it all out. I'll be here when it's over. I'll be here until you're ready to move on after the baby is born. Get it all out."

♥

"Joseph, Reggie. Amy and I had a confrontation with Amy's ex, Tom. He accosted us with the accusation he's the biological father of the child she's carrying. I did as you instructed and told him he had better be right. Amy freaked out, wondering what I meant."

"Did you tell her anything?"

"No, I didn't. I'm following your instructions. I think—no, I know—she's scared and confused. I told Tom I hoped he was right and he needed to get a lawyer."

"Good, I'll proceed. Please don't say or explain anything to Amy. Getting what you want depends on not preparing her."

"Yeah. Just get as early a hearing date as possible."

"Don't worry. My partners know who to call."

Chapter Fourteen

Two weeks later, Amy was deep in analysis and report writing for a client who planned to buy a small regional competitor, which would give the client a broader geographic range and wider array of products. She was particularly excited about the proposal because it had originated from her independent recommendation a year ago at a client outing. She heard a rap on the door and looked up, then smiled and waved Reggie into her office. "Good afternoon. To what do I owe this surprise?"

Reggie shut the door, causing Amy's smile to fade, and said, "We have a court date in one week, Tuesday at 2:00 p.m., in Judge Sabatini Black's chambers. Tom has been served a subpoena. Remember what I've told you: under no circumstances should you say anything. My attorney will not ask you any questions. Tom's might, but my attorney will challenge his request. Since you're my wife, he says the challenge will win."

Amy went to her computer and checked her calendar. "Okay, I'm clear." She typed the info into her computer. "Have you told Margaret you have this meeting?"

"Frankly, no. I asked her to clear my calendar for the day. You'll have to make your way to the courthouse alone. I'm going to arrive with my attorney. You must trust me, Amy. What have I told you?"

"You'll always do what is right for me and my baby, and you'll always be there for me."

"That's almost correct. Our baby, Amy, not just yours. I want you to repeat that over and over every day until the hearing is over."

"What if the hearing goes against us?"

"We'll face that challenge if we must. Joseph is very good at what he does. I'm confident he'll carry the day. Either way, we're having dinner with him and Karen, his wife, at Elio's at seven that night."

♥

LATER THAT WEEK, MARGARET, AMY and Reggie's assistant, came to Amy's office door holding a business card and said, "Excuse me, Amy. There's an attorney at my desk. She first asked for Reggie, but when I told her he was out of the office, she asked to speak with you. I don't know what it's about." She handed the business card to Amy. Looking at the card, Amy felt a sharp kick from her unborn child. The color drained out of her face and she felt dizzy. "Are you alright, Amy?"

"I'm fine. Give me five minutes and bring her back." Amy closed her eyes and breathed deeply. She had dreaded another confrontation caused by the complexities of her arranged marriage, and here it was. Reggie was not here to navigate the potential pitfalls, but she felt she could handle whatever was coming. Amy thought about how she looked. She had tried her best to appear anything but a seven-months-pregnant woman, but nothing worked. This was not the right time or her best condition for meeting her biggest rival for Reggie. Little did Isabella Devoneaux know she would have Reggie back in four months. How could she keep Isabella at bay until the divorce without hurting Reggie's chances to resume his relationship with Isabella? Amy knew Isabella had to be first-class. Everything Reggie had done since their marriage showed he accepted only the best.

Amy was stunned by Isabella's beauty and impeccable presentation. The suit she wore was from Ralph Lauren's tailoring shop. The jewelry was real and just enough to prove she was the real deal.

Isabella walked over to Amy's desk and held out her hand. "Amy, I'm Isabella Devoneaux. It's nice to finally meet you and put a face with a name."

Amy interpreted that comment to mean "You're not so pretty, and I can take Reggie back." Bile rose in her throat. She coughed.

"Ms. Devoneaux, Margaret said you had business with Reggie. How can I be of assistance in his absence?"

"No, my asking for Reggie was to see if he was here. I wanted to see you. I wanted to see the person who beat me out of Reggie's affection, and I wanted to put you on notice I'm not giving up on having a relationship with Reggie."

"Well, isn't that interesting. I'm surprised by you. You are obviously attractive and successful. I'm surprised you feel Reggie's marrying me was some form of rejection of you. I don't know what Reggie has told you—"

"That's just it. He hasn't told me anything. When he sent my birthday present back, there wasn't even a note. He won't take my calls here. His cell phone number isn't working. I get his explanation about ethics, but he and I were good together. Obviously from your condition, the two of you were compatible, and you were careless or conniving. I can't imagine Reggie would like either of those traits. At least I now know you trapped him into marrying you. I'm confident I can win him back." Isabella stood, turned, and walked to the door before Amy could speak.

"Ms. Devoneaux, wait. I thought you and Reggie were close and knew each other well. If you truly knew Reggie, you would know Reggie can't be 'trapped,' as you call it, by anyone or anything. Reggie asked me to marry him. He also knows he is free to terminate the marriage at any time. He chooses not to for two reasons. First, he loves me. Second, he knows I love him with all my heart and soul. He knows I only want his happiness and for him to be proud of his wife. If a divorce would make him happy, I'd give it to him today. Obviously, you don't love him enough to be concerned about his happiness; you just want to be the victor in some mystical struggle for his body. Good day, Ms. Devoneaux. I'll tell Reggie you stopped by." Amy swiveled her chair around and started typing on her computer.

After Isabella left, Amy wondered what part of the conversation she would tell Reggie. Would she admit she'd told Isabella she loved Reggie with all her heart and soul? Was that true? For the second time, she had professed her love for Reggie to someone else without even realizing the words were coming out. She decided she wouldn't tell him about the confrontation. Reggie would be free in four months. Would Isabella wait for that short time? Amy doubted it. Isabella was insecure, even with her beauty and wealth. She needed someone all the time. Amy realized she did too. Tears started flowing. She got up and closed the door and the blinds. How could she ever find someone as kind and generous as Reggie? She knew she couldn't. She tried to think about enjoying the here and now and not contemplate the future divorce sadness. It didn't work.

Chapter Fifteen

At one-thirty the next Tuesday, Amy stood outside the courthouse. She looked at the paper in her hand with the room number and name Judge Sabatini Black on it. She shut her eyes and repeated the mantra of the last week in her mind: Reggie will always do what is right for me and our baby. He will always be there for me.

Amy was sitting alone in the outer office of Judge Black's chambers when Tom and his attorney arrived. He looked at Amy and snickered. She looked down at her hands in her lap. Then she leaned over and picked up a magazine about family law. She wished it was a fashion magazine, but anything was better than looking up and seeing Tom. Her baby chose that time to kick her repeatedly. She knew the cruel smirk Tom had on his face as he saw her sitting there alone. She had seen it many times when he thought he had the upper hand on someone, even her. Where was Reggie? A couple of minutes later, Reggie and his attorney walked in. Amy felt relief. She smiled at him. He didn't smile and turned to speak to his attorney. Her baby kicked again. A chill ran through her body. She repeated Reggie's mantra over and over silently to herself, but she still felt an overwhelming sense of aloneness. It took all of her willpower to not cry. She returned to reading some story in the magazine about family law.

Finally the judge came out, shook hands all around, and escorted them into his chambers. The room was large. Sitting in front of a double window was a massive desk with stacks of file folders like two pillars on top. To the right of the desk was a young man in front of a small typewriter instrument with a roll of paper fed through it from a box on the floor. The paper, once through the machine, was caught in another box attached to the back. Five leather chairs were arranged around the front and left sides of the desk. One chair was off to the side, while the other four were arranged in front in pairs. The walls were lined with law books and others. Amy glanced at the ones behind where she was to sit and noticed book titles about families. The floor was covered with a thick green wall-to-wall sound-dampening carpet. All the lighting in the room came from the window and strategically placed table lamps. The aura was one of seriousness and respectability. Judge Black motioned for Amy to sit in the chair off to the side. He pointed to the two pairs of chairs for Reggie and Tom and their attorneys. Then he took his seat, nodded to the stenographer, and said, "Lady and gentlemen, we are here to settle in a legal and private way the parentage of the fetus being carried by Mrs. Amy Boykin." Hearing the words, Amy felt weak, and the room started spinning until she focused her mind. The judge continued, "Since this hearing was requested by Mr. Boykin, he and his attorney will make pleadings first." Amy, wide-eyed, looked at Reggie. He looked out the window behind the judge.

Reggie's attorney spoke next. "If it pleases Your Honor, my client is requesting adjudication because Tom Edwards has told multiple people in a public setting that he is the father of Mrs. Boykin's fetus. In looking into the situation, we estimate at least fifty individuals were the recipients of these claims. If the claims are true, and there is a question as to their veracity, Mr. Boykin wishes the court to find so, and confirm Mr. Edwards is therefore financially responsible for the child's prenatal, delivery, and pediatric care through the age of eighteen. Further, he requests the judge consider giving Mr. Edwards joint custody of the child, with required father-child overnight visits on Tuesdays and Thursdays, every other weekend, and six weeks in the summer. Finally, my client requests the court set monthly child support as a percentage of Mr. Edwards's income to be paid until the child is eighteen."

Amy sat like she was strapped into an electric chair. Her arms were tight against the chair, her back rigid against the chair back, her feet flat on the floor, her legs and thighs squeezed together tightly. Every time Reggie's attorney said another sentence, she flinched and felt the baby kick. Even though her eyes were riveted on Reggie and she wasn't believing what she was hearing, she could see Tom, in her line of sight, looking from her to Reggie and back again like he was at some diabolical tennis match. His sneer had deepened, delighting in the pain Amy couldn't hide, as he thought about the wedge he was driving between her and Reggie. Amy wanted to scream, but Reggie had been emphatic that under no circumstances was she to say anything. Even as she heard Reggie's attorney demand that Tom, who Reggie knew was the father of her child, accept parental costs and responsibility for the child, her mind was involuntarily repeating Reggie's mantra: remember, I would never do anything to hurt you or our child. He had lied. The whole scheme was a lie. Had he grown tired of her in just a few months? Why hadn't he mentioned the costs? She was already paying the doctor bills out of her own money. Why hadn't he said something when he proposed this sham marriage? Her thoughts bounced like a pinball from Reggie having a change of heart to his wanting out of this marriage early. Oh God, she was going to be all alone. There was no one else. No lifelong girlfriends, no Granny, no parents she could rely on. Even Helen would be gone. Alone—her biggest fear. For a moment, unconsciously her left hand lifted from the chair and touched her locket. She silently pleaded for her granny's help.

"Mr. Edwards, what response do you or your attorney have concerning these requests?"

"Your Honor, I'll respond for my client. We find these requests ludicrous. Mr. Boykin is the husband, and he is responsible for the expenses of his wife."

"Mr. Edwards, have you publicly stated that you are the father of Mrs. Boykin's fetus?"

Tom turned to his attorney, and they conferred. The attorney said, "Your Honor, my client does not have a clear memory; however, it's possible he may have inferred such in speaking with mutual friends of his and Mrs. Boykin's prior to her marriage." Amy was looking at Tom now, her crushing disappointment with Reggie turning into white-hot anger at both: Reggie for deceiving her into this situation, and Tom for being the weakling who wanted to kill their unborn child.

"Counsel, thank you for trying to obscure the facts. I'll ask Mr. Edwards again and request a yes-or-no answer. Did you at any time say to more than one person that you were the father of Mrs. Boykin's fetus? Yes or no, Mr. Edwards?"

"Er . . . yes, Your Honor."

"On what basis did you make this claim?"

"Uh, we were having sex during the time Mrs. Boykin likely got pregnant."

"Mr. Edwards, what proof do you have that you were the only person Mrs. Boykin was having sex with?" Amy coughed, trying to suppress the bile rising in her throat. Her breath came in short, hyperventilated gasps. She didn't feel the pain in her hands, as her fingernails dug deep into the chair's padded arms. Her legs involuntarily trembled as she tried to keep them flat on the rug. She could hardly see through her tears. She wanted to get up and run from the office. She thanked God this was not in a courtroom where reporters and the world would hear this testimony.

"None, Your Honor."

"So, you believe honestly that you are the father, but you don't know that for sure."

"That's correct, Your Honor."

The judge turned to Reggie's attorney and asked, "Counselor, do you have any estimates of the cost for prenatal, delivery, and post-birth pediatric care until the child is one year old?"

"Yes, Your Honor. The prenatal care is estimated at fifteen thousand dollars; the delivery for the physician and hospital is estimated at forty thousand dollars, assuming no complications, and ten thousand for one year post-birth care."

The judge used a pencil to add up the amounts. He looked at the four men sitting across from him and said, "That totals sixty-five thousand dollars.

Mr. Edwards, as the father of this fetus, you have a responsibility to support your unborn child, and, in the future, your child until age eighteen. Since you claim to be the father, I lean to ruling you are responsible for these costs, and, after the child is born, grant you joint custody of the child, including twice-weekly overnight visits, every-other-weekend responsibility, and a period of time each summer, not less than six weeks, with a sliding child support amount based upon your earnings each year. Since there seems to be a question as to the paternity of the fetus, I want to give you two alternatives: (a) submit to a DNA test so that your responsibility can be established in fact, or (b) sign a stipulation and finding that you renounce for now and any time in the future any claim to parental rights and parental responsibility in fact. Counselor, would you like to confer with your client in private to explain the ramifications of each alternative?"

"Yes, Your Honor."

The judge picked up his phone and spoke to his assistant. Tom and his attorney were directed to a side room. While they were gone, the judge swiveled his chair around and busied himself with folders on his credenza. Reggie and his attorney talked quietly among themselves. Amy realized this was the moment of truth. If Tom came back agreeing to the DNA test, he would win, and her life with this pretend marriage would essentially be over. Everyone would know the truth. Importantly, everyone would think she had tricked Reggie into marrying her. Amy's character and training burst through the emotions of disappointment with Reggie and disgust and contempt for Tom. She resolved to do whatever was necessary to protect Reggie. He had done his best to help her, and she would be forever grateful that he had kept her from having an abortion. She would always owe him that. She began planning her future. She would get a studio apartment again. She would get a divorce earlier than she and Reggie had planned, but she would still have her partnership because a divorce is not the same as being pregnant and unwed. They could say it was an honest mistake that the baby turned out to be Tom's. She didn't know if Reggie would say that, but he was such a stand-up guy, she was confident he would. Even as her brain cleared, her heart was still breaking at her misreading of Reggie's intentions. Still, when she heard the door to the room open, she was thankful she had put on a panty liner. She dug her fingernails into the leather arms of the chair. Tom and his attorney took their seats, and the judge turned back to the room.

He looked at Tom and his counselor. "Well, what is your decision, Mr. Edwards?"

"If it pleases Your Honor, my client has decided to sign the stipulation and finding to close this matter out." Tom sneered at Amy as these words were uttered. The judge opened the file on his desk and pulled out two pages. He handed them to Tom's attorney, who scanned the pages and gave Tom his folio and pen to use when signing. He signed and gave everything back to the attorney, who then handed the pages to the judge, who countersigned the papers.

"Counselors, the court will process these findings and send both attorneys a certified copy."

At that moment, Reggie's attorney spoke up, "Your Honor, I'd like to request these proceedings be sealed since it will benefit neither side for them to be made public."

The judge looked at Tom's attorney and raised his eyebrows. "My client agrees, Your Honor," Tom's attorney responded.

"So be it." With that, Tom jumped up, smiled cruelly at Amy, and walked out of the room, not waiting for his attorney. Reggie and Joseph and Tom's attorney shook hands with the judge and each other. Amy just sat there, completely drained. Reggie went over to her. She did not look at him. He took her by the arm and peeled her out of the chair. They walked out of the room with Reggie supporting her and stopped to speak to Joseph in the reception area. Joseph and Reggie hugged each other. Joseph turned to Amy, but Reggie squeezed his arm and shook his head.

"Joseph, we look forward to dinner tonight. See you at seven," Reggie said.

Amy still wouldn't look at Reggie when they were outside. "I want to go home and be alone," she said.

"I understand." Reggie said as he texted for a Lyft car. He stayed with her until the car arrived.

♥

AMY SAT NUMBLY IN THE car. The tears had stopped when Reggie peeled her out of the chair in the judge's chambers. She held her locket tightly. "Granny," she whispered, not really caring if the driver heard her or not. "How could I have been so wrong? I knew he didn't love me and I didn't love him, but I thought this arranged marriage might save my career, keep me from killing this child growing inside of me, and help his career as well. He seemed so nice every day. How could I have missed the signs that he was tired of me and my baby? I believed him when he said he would never hurt us. Granny, how could I be so wrong? You said I'd know what unconditional love was when I met the right person. I was beginning to understand what you meant." Amy's tears began to fall. She turned her head to look out the window so the driver wouldn't see her crying. She felt so betrayed and mortified that she was responsible for this predicament. Granny, how could I have trusted him? she asked silently. Granny, please help me, please. I'm so alone. I need you, Granny. Oh God, I'm scared of being all alone. Through her tears Amy realized the Lyft car was slowing and stopping in front of her building. She quickly dried her tears so the doorman wouldn't see her crying. Breathing deeply, she composed herself.

Upstairs, she sat at the dining table. She wanted to pack her things but realized she had no place to go. She'd call the apartment company tomorrow from the office. Maybe she could afford a one-bedroom with a view of the Hudson and within walking distance of the office. She knew her first concern was confronting Reggie and making sure she paid Joseph's fee for the assassination of her that he'd orchestrated today. Reggie could go to dinner with him and celebrate saving sixty-five thousand dollars and getting out of their arranged marriage. Her anger grew until she looked over at the bookcases. She thought about the intense pleasure she had, and, she thought, Reggie had on their book hunts together. She realized he was a good person and was crushed by his rejection, wondering what she had done to turn him from a caring person to someone who wanted her gone. She heard the elevator doors open and close and a key slide into the apartment door lock.

"Hello. Feeling better?" Reggie said as he came through the door.

"I'm fine. What I want to know is what Joseph's fee was for that performance today." Amy's tone was caustic and hard. Reggie loosened his tie and unbuttoned his collar. He smiled and went to the kitchen.

"I'm getting a bottle of water. Want one?"

"No, thank you. I want to know what Joseph charged for his services. I also want to make it clear that I've been paying for all the medical expenses associated with my pregnancy and the birth of my child."

Reggie spun around. "Did you forget what I asked you to remember through this whole episode?" he snapped. "Let's also get another matter clarified. You just said 'my' child. The baby is our child. Someone else may be the biological creator of the fetus, but I'm the one who is nurturing the mother and fetus."

"Talk is cheap. Actions speak louder than words. Now, what did he charge?" She held her Montblanc pen poised above a blank check.

"He charged nothing. Joseph and I have a special relationship. I told you he was my roommate in undergraduate school. He was instrumental in getting me through my time in Crozet. And I have helped him during times when he was at a loss. He and Karen wouldn't be married today without my help. While our schedules are such that we don't see each other much, we talk at least weekly. What he did today was just part of our love for each other."

Amy felt sick to her stomach out of regret for being so harsh. Reggie's calm demeanor said more than his words. Still, she was disappointed that Reggie hadn't told her what the hearing was going to be like.

"Why didn't you warn me what was going to go down?"

"Joseph told me not to. He had investigated Tom and felt we were never going to convince him to leave us alone if he thought that was what we wanted. Tom had to go away from this afternoon believing he had won and hurt both of us. The whole exercise hinged on his signing away his parental rights. That's why I told you we could lose. That's why it was important for you to not sit in the room casually, knowing what was going to unfold. You are a good person and can't play-act emotions. Tom signed the paper for three reasons, all of which were designed by Joseph: first, he thought it would leave you alone without support; second, he felt he had driven a wedge between us and ruined our marriage; and finally, it got him off the hook of supporting you and our child for the next eighteen-plus years. Without believing he was crushing both of our lives, he would not have signed."

Amy suddenly recognized the masterful sequence of events a brilliant lawyer had orchestrated and felt shame for doubting Reggie.

"Is there anything else you want to know?"

Impulsively, Amy said, "Yeah. Who is Jenny?"

Reggie looked down at the table and in a low voice asked, "Jenny who?"

"I don't know. That's what I'm asking you. Is she an old girl-friend? Will she pop up in the future like Tom did? Obviously, she's important to you. You sound like you're crying and calling out to her. If you still love her, I'll understand. If you want to see her while we're married, I'll understand."

"Jenny will not pop up, as you say." Reggie looked at his watch. "I'm going to go have a power nap, take a shower, and be ready for the car to pick us up at six thirty. Have you been to Elio's?"

"No."

"It's the best Italian restaurant in the city. It's over on Second Avenue between Eighty-Fourth and Eighty-Fifth. They have a customer mix of celebrities and locals. Joseph and his family dine there every week since he lives close by. The manager and staff are highly professional. Joseph has a favorite server named Walter who has been there for around thirty years. The food is outstanding. If you've never been and enjoy meat, I suggest you try the veal piccata limone. If you're interested, we can share their chopped salad, and if it's on the menu, their fresh bread pudding."

"What are you ordering?"

"If they have them, soft-shell crabs. If not, the dover sole or fluke." With that, Reggie got up and went to his room.

Amy sat there drained of her anger and mad at herself for doubting Reggie. She still felt unanchored to anything. Her pregnancy was temporary. Her marriage was temporary. She couldn't believe she'd gotten herself into this situation. And she realized he hadn't answered who Jenny was.

♥

REGGIE AND AMY ENTERED ELIO'S and were met by the manager, Jerry.

"Reservations?" he asked, looking from Reggie to Amy. She was looking around the crowded restaurant. It was obviously not a tourist hub. Most of the patrons looked like neighborhood residents, some with children in tow, almost all relaxed and comfortable, almost like being in their own dining room. In front, in the corner, was a celebrity. Amy squeezed Reggie's hand to get his attention.

"We're meeting Joseph Harrington," Reggie said, ignoring Amy for a minute.

"Oh, yes. Mr. Harrington said he had guests coming. Please follow Luca to their regular table." Luca led them over to the second right-side table in the main dining area. Joseph stood and hugged Reggie and offered his hand to Amy.

"Amy, I'm sorry. I know that was brutal, but it was the only way to accomplish our objective. I hope you understand," Joseph said as he and Amy shook hands.

Amy put on her best professional smile and responded, "Yes, Joseph, your assessment is correct. Not to worry, I'll forgive you in, er, fifty or sixty years." She winked at him. All four of them laughed. Then she turned to Reggie and said, "Did you see who was at that front table in the corner?"

Reggie turned to Joseph and looked quizzically at him. "Oh yes, he eats here just about every night he's in town. A great guy. The regulars leave him alone so he can enjoy his meal in peace. Now I don't know about you, but I'm starved. Let's get Walter over to order some wine and food. He just got back from his month in Croatia, his native country. He and the entire front-of-house staff are what make the Elio's experience so special—along with the food, of course."

Amy wondered how she would fit in with Reggie, Joseph, and Karen being friends for so long, and she, very much a loner, being the outsider at the table. To her surprise, Joseph and Karen treated her as if she had been part of the group for years. She was let in on every inside comment that only the three of them would really understand. Toward the end of the evening, both Reggie and Joseph excused themselves to go downstairs to the restroom. When they were out of earshot, Karen turned to Amy and said, "Joseph tells me you're focused on your career and don't have any close girlfriends. If you allow me, I'd like us to be friends—close friends.

"You probably don't understand yet just how close these two guys we're married to are. Fortunately, I've been lucky enough to love one of them and see how strong a bond is possible between really caring people. When Joseph and I were having our first child, I had the support of my now-deceased mother and some good friends. Being pregnant and having a baby is not easy for anyone, but it must be even tougher without other women to support you. If you'll allow me, I'd like to be your support. I know Reggie—he'll do what any guy can do, but it's not the same as being close to another woman who has been through the ordeal of birthing and adjusting to motherhood. I don't want to intrude, but I'm here if you want some support."

Amy brushed away a tear. "Forgive me, I seem to cry at the drop of a hat these days. Karen, I'd appreciate it more than you can know, having another woman to talk to. You're right, Reggie is wonderful, but there are things I can't say or ask him about." Amy took deep breaths, smiled, and leaned over and hugged Karen.

Karen pulled her card from her pocketbook and gave it to Amy. "Wait, let me put my unlisted cell number on the back." She retrieved a pen from her pocketbook. Amy did the same, and they traded cards. "Our special guys talk at least weekly. Let's try to do that, too. Maybe Joseph and Reggie can arrange for the four of us and our two kids to have a Sunday in the park playdate." Karen's brow wrinkled and she said, "On second thought, we shouldn't have that play date until after you have your child. Otherwise, you may put your baby up for adoption after experiencing life with small children." The two of them burst into raucous laughter. The guys returned to find other patrons looking around and staring at the two women.

"What is so hilarious?" Reggie asked, putting his hand on Amy's shoulder.

"We were just plotting how Amy is going to get back at you for the condition she's in," Karen said between breaths, and the women had another round of laughter.

After saying goodbye to Walter, Luca, Jerry, and the rest of the staff nearby, the four went out on Second Avenue, where Reggie and Amy had a car waiting. Joseph extended his hand to Amy. She grabbed his arm and pulled him in for a hug. With her mouth close to his ear, she said, "Thank you." She turned to Karen, hugged her, and said she would call at the first of the week. Reggie hugged both of his friends and waved as they walked down Second Avenue toward their apartment.

In the car, Reggie and Amy sat quietly, processing the day and the evening, holding hands. Amy looked over at Reggie, who had his head back and his eyes closed. She turned and looked out the window, thinking about how her world had vaporized by five, reappeared by six, and solidified in a human group of pure love for each other. For a fleeting moment, she realized she was anchored like she had been when Granny was alive. She was loved by complete strangers just because she had been chosen to be a part of their group by one of its members. Reality overwhelmed these secure thoughts. Would Karen take her calls when she and Reggie were divorced? There wouldn't be any more dinners at Elio's, that was for sure. She would be all alone again, raising her child. The child was the only happy part of the reality check. She pulled Reggie's hand over so that it was touching her thigh. She wanted to hold him close so he knew she now understood what he had done for her a second time. Touching her locket, she knew what she needed to do even though there would be a divorce. As she looked straight ahead and moved his hand, Reggie opened his eyes to look at her. A half-smile appeared on his face.

Chapter Sixteen

my's emotions swung constantly from happiness that she had only five weeks before her baby was due to abject fear at being a single mother shortly after the birth. It was late as she tossed from one side to another, tucking a shallow pillow between her abdomen and the mattress. As she closed her eyes for the third time, she heard a piercing cry. Jumping out of bed, she went to the hall and listened at Reggie's door. He was crying and saying, "Jenny, no!"

She went into the room and saw him on his stomach, gripping the sheets. She climbed into the bed and pulled him to her, holding him and whispering in his ear, "Shh, Reggie, I'm here. Everything is alright." She lay on her back and rested his head on her swollen breasts. He put his arm across her belly without waking up. She stroked his hair. He continued to sleep but stopped crying out and developed a regular breathing rhythm. She closed her eyes and slept peacefully.

The next morning, Reggie opened his eyes before Amy. He bolted up and looked at her.

"Good morning," she said shyly, pulling the sheet up to her chin.

"What happened? What are you doing here?" Reggie asked.

"I'm sorry. You were having a particularly bad nightmare, so I came in to help you. The only thing I could think of was to hold you to calm you down. You were crying out for Jenny to not do something or leave you. I didn't mean to intrude. I'll go back to my room."

Reggie took her hand. "Amy, I'm sorry about my stupid nightmares. You shouldn't have to be going through this. Thank you." He got up and said, "I'll make some coffee in a couple of minutes. Would you like an egg and an English muffin? I'm so sorry and embarrassed."

"Sure. It'll take me thirty minutes to get cleaned up and close enough to being ready." She got up and stood there in her loose nightgown with her hair askew and barefoot. Briefly smiling, she turned and waddled out of his room. She felt good that she had been able to show him as much kindness as he showed her daily. Neither of them mentioned the incident the rest of the day or thereafter. As usual, they walked to the office holding hands.

♥

SEVERAL DAYS LATER, REGGIE STEPPED into an elevator leaving a client's office. As the doors closed, he heard a familiar voice: "Good afternoon, Reggie." He looked to his left and saw Isabella.

"Good afternoon, Isabella. Client meeting?"

"Yes. I assume the same for you?"

"Yes."The elevator doors opened and the occupants emerged.

"You have a minute?" Isabella asked.

"Actually, I'm in a rush."

"Don't worry, Reggie, I'm not going to hit on you. I assume your wife told you I went to see her."

"You did? When? She didn't say anything about it."

"A couple of weeks ago. You're a lucky guy."

"What do you mean?"

"I told Amy—that's her name, right?"

"Yes."

"I told her I wasn't giving up on having a relationship with you, along with some other crude remarks. One-alpha-female-to-another garbage. What a dope I was. She told me she loved you so much that if it would make you happy to be with me, she would give you a divorce right then, that day. It wasn't until later that it hit me. I've never loved someone so much that I'd suffer losing them if it made them happy. Thanks to her, I've come to understand that kind of unconditional love. I haven't found it, but at least now I know what I'm looking for. I wish you, Amy, and your soon-to-be-born child much happiness." She reached up and kissed him on the cheek.

"Isabella, thank you. Amy didn't tell me you had seen her. She is special. I wish you much happiness as well." They walked out together and parted, Isabella getting into a hired car and Reggie turning to walk to his office. He thought about what Isabella had said. Amy not mentioning Isabella's visit was telling. Did she say what she did to Isabella because she meant it, or because she just wanted to hold Isabella away for a few more months until the divorce? Their relationship had evolved into something pleasant, but she'd never given him a hint that she wanted to tear up their contract. Did he want to tear it up? He didn't know.

There was no question his aching emptiness was lessened. His nightmares were less frequent. His regrets were less frequent. Happy moments and satisfaction were more frequent. More than anything, the morning he had awakened from sleeping next to Amy with his arm across her body, the peaceful feeling that had overcome him had been wonderful. It felt right. Her kindness and caring for his well-being without implying she deserved some payback was the kind of unconditional love she talked about. He knew there wasn't much time left before the Christmas Gala, where she would be made a partner. After that, they would need to sit down and work out the details of the divorce. What would life without Amy be like? It had only been six and a half months since their marriage, almost seven months that were mostly happy times. He decided not to think about it. He had learned at Crozet to live for the present and enjoy every day.

Chapter Seventeen

Amy's pregnancy was nearly over. The office Christmas Gala was ten days away. The firm would name new partners at the party. Reggie's charade marriage scheme to save her partnership appeared to have worked. She shook her head, trying to dispel the negative thoughts of their pending divorce. She had made her decision: she would keep the child and figure out a way to support both of them. Professionally, Reggie and Amy had fed off each other's experiences and abilities, becoming an analytical powerhouse able to help partners on many projects, but her mind returned to the cloud on their horizon. Amy and Reggie both realized separately the code word for backing off, *divorce*, had never been spoken by either of them. After a long day at the office, Amy had gone to bed immediately after eating dinner and helping Reggie wash the dishes.

Around eleven, she came out of her bedroom with her coat on. Reggie, who was sitting on the sofa, reading a history book, looked at her. "Where are you going? It's nearly eleven, cold outside, and threatening rain. If you go out there, you'll catch a cold, and you're just weeks away from delivery."

"I need some chocolate mint ice cream. I won't be out there but a few minutes."

"No, you won't. If you want chocolate mint ice cream, I'll go get it."

"No, I'm going."

"Amy Boykin, getting craving-food is in the purview of the soon-to-be dad, not the pregnant mom-to-be." He got up, slipped on his shoes, mussed her hair, grabbed his jacket, and went out the door before she could protest.

Thirty minutes later Reggie hadn't returned. She looked at her phone and thought about texting him but decided not to. He was probably talking to someone. Her mind jumped to Isabella, but she quickly dismissed the negative thought. He probably had to go to a second store to get the ice cream. Her phone rang and startled her. It was Reggie calling. "If you can't find it, that's okay," she said when answering.

"Is this Mrs. Reginald Boykin?" a strange voice asked. Amy felt a pang of fear shoot through her body.

"Yes, is there something wrong?"

"Mrs. Boykin, this is Officer Custer of the NYPD. Your husband has been in an accident. He is unconscious and being transported to Lenox Hill Hospital on Seventy-Seventh between Park and Lexington Ave." There was silence on the line. "Mrs. Boykin, are you there?"

"Oh, God, no. Is he alright? Can I speak to him? What happened?"

"Ma'am, your husband was hit by a bicyclist as he was crossing the street. He hit his head on the curb and is unconscious. He is alive. He left in the ambulance five minutes ago. You'll have to talk to the hospital to get a status update. His phone will be at the precinct station on West Thirty-Third Street if you want to pick it up in the morning."

"Thanks for calling, officer."

Amy's hands were trembling so badly, she dropped her phone on the table. She knew she had to get to the hospital. Where was their marriage license? She needed something to prove who she was. She knew the insurance information from work. Forcing herself to calm down, she started prioritizing her actions. First get dressed. She went and found a dress, flat shoes, and a coat. She went back to the table and picked up the phone. Unable to dial with her hands shaking, she put the phone on the table and rested her wrist on the table. Opening the phone, she punched the number for Lyft. After ordering a car, she thought about calling Reggie's parents. She decided not to and put the phone in her coat pocket and grabbed her purse.

In the car, she realized she should call Reggie's parents. His father answered. "Mr. Boykin, this is Amy. Reggie has been in an accident. I'm on the way to Lenox Hill Hospital now. I don't know anything except he's unconscious. I'll call you back when I know something more."

"Hold on, Amy, don't hang up!" A few seconds later Helen Boykin came on the line.

"Amy, how bad are Reggie's injuries?"

"I don't know. The policeman said he was hit by a bicyclist in the crosswalk."

"When did this happen?"

"About thirty minutes ago."

"Why was he out at this time of night and you not with him?"

Amy started sobbing. "He went to get me some ice cream. It's all my fault!"

"Calm down, Amy. Reggie needs all of us to be able to help him through this crisis. What hospital is he in?"

"Lenox Hill Hospital, on Seventy-Seventh between Park and Lexington. I'm on my way now."

"I'll be there in the morning. Stay strong and calm. Call me when you find out anything, anything at all."

"I will. He's got to be alright. He can't die," she wailed, holding tightly to her locket.

♥

REGGIE WAS IN THE EMERGENCY room for less than thirty minutes. They rushed him to the operating room to relieve the pressure from bleeding on the brain. An hour and a half after arriving at the hospital, he was taken to a room. Because of her condition, Amy was allowed to be in the room with him. She sat in a chair next to the bed, holding his right hand. His left wrist and hand were in a cast. His head was completely bandaged except for his face. A doctor came in shortly after.

"You must be Mrs. Boykin. I'm Dr. Steven Shapiro. I'm your husband's attending physician."

"Please tell me he's going to be alright," Amy pleaded.

"Your husband has an excellent chance to make a full recovery. I don't know how long he will be unconscious. You may consider talking to him. We really don't know if he can hear you; however, studies indicate it doesn't hurt and may be beneficial."

"When will he wake up?"

"We don't know. Every patient is different. My estimation is sometime midday, maybe sooner if he hears you. I'll be here in the morning around eight. Don't worry too much."

When Dr. Shapiro left, Amy sat holding Reggie's hand and started talking, "Reggie Boykin, if you don't wake up soon, I'll never speak to you again. You infuriate me. I've never met anyone who was as perfect in every way. Please wake up Reggie. The truth is, I love you more than I thought I could love anyone in my life. I need you, even if I know we're going to get divorced in a few months. When I think about how you knew what I was going to do, and you were willing to put your life on hold for me, I don't know how I can ever repay your kindness and concern. If I knew how to get in touch with Jenny, I'd call her, tell her how much you love her, and request—no, demand—she come and make you happy. You deserve to be happy, and I've done nothing except bring you grief and unhappiness. I'll do whatever I can to make you happy, I promise."

Amy kissed Reggie's hand. "I just kissed your hand. I don't know if you could feel it. That's the second time I've kissed you. It seems I don't have the courage to kiss you when you're awake, but I want to kiss you for hours. I want to hold you. I want to feel you inside me after our baby is born. I love you with all my heart and soul. Please wake up and get well so I can know you're alright." She adjusted herself in the chair with her head on his hand and closed her eyes.

♥

"Amy, Amy," Helen Boykin said softly, putting her hand on Amy's shoulder. Amy jerked awake and looked up at Helen and the suitcase next to her chair.

"Helen, what are you doing here?" It was then she saw a man, not Reggie's father, looking at Reggie's eyes and the monitors. "Oh, God, what's happening? Has Reggie taken a turn for the worse?" She grabbed his hand and held on tight. At that moment, Dr. Shapiro walked into the room.

The man looking at Reggie turned and smiled at Dr. Shapiro. "Hello, Steven."

"Good lord, Mort, what are you doing here?"

"Steven, let me introduce you to Mrs. Helen Boykin. Helen, this is Dr. Steven Shapiro. He was a Boykin Scholar every year of medical school—without a doubt, the best student I've ever had the privilege of teaching. Steven, Helen is the medical school board chair. Her family also endowed the Boykin Brain Medicine Chair I occupy and the scholarship you won. She asked if I would come over this morning to consult with Reggie's doctor. If I had known it was you, I would have eased her fears."

"Mrs. Boykin, thank you for all you do for the medical school. Your son has an excellent probability of a full recovery. Mort, let's go to the central station and I'll fill you in on Mr. Boykin's condition."

"Mort, when you're ready, the car is downstairs and will take you back to Teterboro. The plane is standing by and expecting you. I'm going to stay for a few days," Helen said.

"Fine. I'm glad everything looks good. I'll get a briefing from Steven and then head back."

Helen and Mort hugged, and he left with Dr. Shapiro. Amy continued to hold Reggie's hand, dumbfounded by what she had just heard and watched.

"Amy, would it be an imposition if I stayed with you while here?" Amy realized she had to come up with a reason why all her clothes were in the guest room.

"Oh, Helen, of course you can stay with us. I want to tell you, a week ago I moved into the guest room so Reggie could have a peaceful night of sleep. I'll move back into our bedroom. It will be nice to have you there." The two of them turned to Reggie. Amy said to him, "Reggie, your mother is here. She'll visit us until you're better."

Helen went to the left side of the bed, touched Reggie's cheek, and leaned down to kiss him. "Get better, son. I can't lose another child."

Amy was startled and confused by her comment. She realized Helen might know where Reggie's former girlfriend was. Perhaps Helen could convince her to come and help Reggie.

"Helen, Reggie has nightmares about an old girlfriend. I think he's still in love with her, and it might help him if she could come and let him know she's here." Amy couldn't control the tears flowing down her cheeks. Helen came around the bed, pulled another chair over, and put her arms around Amy.

"Amy, I don't know who you're talking about. I do know my son loves you, not someone else. Who do you think it is?"

"He calls out to Jenny when he has these nightmares."

Helen shut her eyes and took a deep breath. "Amy, Reggie hasn't told you about Jenny?"

"He won't talk about her. The couple of times I asked him, he deflected my question and changed the subject. I just want him happy. He deserves to be happy. If she can make him happy, I'll give him his freedom."

"Amy, Amy, you need to understand about Jenny. For years, Reggie's father and I tried to have children. We just couldn't. Then I did become pregnant. It turned out I was going to have twins. The girl came first. We named her Jenny. Even though she was only two minutes older than Reggie, from the very beginning she assigned herself the big-sister role. The two of them were inseparable until they went to college. They both went to the University of Virginia, but he was in a fraternity and she was in a sorority. During their sophomore year, Jenny started seriously dating a young man from Richmond, Virginia. She became pregnant, told the young man, and he told her that was her problem, not his. He broke up with her. She didn't want to tell us or Reggie about her dilemma. She decided to get an abortion.

"After the procedure, she went into a deep depression. Reggie knew something was wrong, but she wouldn't tell him. We tried to get her to see a doctor, but she wouldn't go." Helen's tears flowed down her cheeks. While still holding Reggie's hand with her left hand, Amy reached over and took Helen's hands in her right. "Jenny finally couldn't handle the situation and took her own life. We were all devastated, but Reggie more so than anyone. He left school, went to Crozet, Virginia, and spent a year and a half trying to understand and shake his depression from his sister's death."

"I had no idea. I thought he was upset over a former girl-friend. Oh, the grief you and your family have had. What a horrible situation to go through," Amy said.

Helen opened her purse and took out her handkerchief to wipe her eyes. "Life has many twists and turns, some good and some not so good. Reggie's father and I still have him. You brought back the Reggie we knew before Jenny's death. Soon, we'll have a grandchild. We don't dwell on what might have been. We focus on what is and what will be. Now, if you're okay here alone with Reggie, I'll call for a car and go to the apartment and lie down."

Amy stood and went over to the windowsill where she had left her pocketbook. She retrieved her keys and gave them to Helen. "When Reggie wakes up, I'll text you." She hugged Helen and held on for longer than necessary, feeling guilty for deceiving this wonderful woman. What would Helen think when the baby was born and she and Reggie divorced? Reggie's parents would be hurt again. At least Reggie would be free to be with Isabella or meet someone he could truly love.

After Helen and Dr. Shapiro left, Amy went back to holding Reggie's hand and talking to him. "Reginald Andrew Boykin the Fourth, this is Mrs. The Fourth speaking to you. Now I know why you were so kind and determined to keep me from having an abortion. I can't imagine the pain you must have endured when you lost your sister. You saved me from doing what I knew I would regret for the rest of my life. You can't hear me, but I want you to know I love you. I love you with my whole heart and soul. I will keep my end of our bargain and give you a divorce, and I'll make it easy for you, but I will always love you. Before our divorce, I want to show you how much by being a real wife, in every way. I'll do anything for you."

♥

FIRST THERE WAS BLACKNESS. HE didn't know where he was or why he was there. He could barely hear a voice fading in and out. He knew he needed to concentrate on the voice. Was it Jenny? He wasn't sure. Then the gaps between the words began to be filled in by more words. He realized the voice was not Jenny. Who, then? A pain shot through his left arm about the time his eyes fluttered open, and he recognized Amy's voice saying, "I'll do anything for you."

"Anything?" Reggie whispered, with his eyes trying to open.

Amy stood up, still holding his hand, and kissed him passionately. "Anything, for you, my love." She continued to kiss his face, his eyes, and his cheeks. Her tears smeared on his face. He smiled.

"I'm sorry I didn't get you the chocolate mint ice cream."

"All I want is you. Your mother told me about Jenny. Your mother is here. She went to the apartment to freshen up. I promised I would text her when you woke up."

"Where is she staying?"

"In the guest room."

"Great, that means you're sleeping with me."

"I'll sleep with you every night until we get our agreed-to divorce."

"You said you would do anything. Did you mean it?"

"Yes, I did and do. Anything."

"Well, Mrs. The Fourth, what I want from you is to not get a divorce. I love you with my whole being. I know what I'm going to say is contrary to what we do every day, putting together facts and figures to logically come up with intelligent, rational decisions. But I truly believe Jenny sent you to me to release my suffering and pain from losing her. Jenny was not just my big sister. She was an extension of me. We were one. How she slipped into the state of mind she did is not comprehensible to me. She should have known I'd stay by her side no matter what.

"From her death until we were married, I felt an aching emptiness that couldn't be filled. I felt I had let her down. I know that's illogical, but I knew something was bothering her and didn't press the issue. After her death, I was overcome with guilt because I didn't go the extra yard to console and support her. That's why I was at the doctor's office that morning. I know Jenny pushed me to be there. To offer you the third option she didn't have. You're so much like her—I didn't realize how much until we started living together. You've healed me. She knew you would. I love you in ways words can't describe. I can't even think about losing you."

"Well, I guess I'll just be Mrs. The Fourth for the rest of our lives if you'll have me."

"One day, perhaps you'll put me next to your heart with your granny," Reggie whispered.

"You're already there, my love." She opened the locket and held it so he could see his picture on the right side. "I knew after our dinner at Elio's that I loved you unconditionally, and, even when we got our divorce, I'd still love you unconditionally. I always want you and Granny close to me."

Reggie smiled and closed his eyes.

Amy was texting Reggie's mother. She pushed the call button so the nurse could call Dr. Shapiro. She turned back to Reggie and said, "Open your eyes so I can see I wasn't dreaming, then you can go back to sleep, my darling." Reggie did as he was told.

Chapter Eighteen

Helen, Reggie, and Amy sat in the living room of their apartment. "You two look like you swallowed the canaries."

"We think so," said Reggie. He and Amy were sitting on the sofa holding hands. Reggie still had a buzz cut and his left arm was in a sling. They had both been named partners at the firm's holiday party the night before. As the senior associate, Amy would almost inevitably be named a partner, but Reggie's elevation to partner was a surprise to both of them. His work with securing the Oatley engagement, his teamwork with Amy, and his initiative over the last six months helping younger associates were cited as the principal reasons for the promotion.

"Mother, we'd like to celebrate with you over dinner at Daniel's."

"That's wonderful. I accept." Her face turned businesslike. "I need some favors from the two of you."

"Sure, Helen. What can we do?" Amy said, squeezing Reggie's hand.

"Boykin Properties just sold an apartment building in Ohio, and we want to do a 1031 exchange. This morning, while you two new partners were working, I went upstairs to the twelfth floor and looked at a four-bed, four-bath apartment. The price was perfect for us to do the 1031. With the rent laws in New

York City, I'm hesitant to put the unit on the rental market. If the two of you are agreeable, Boykin Properties will lease you the unit for the same rent you're paying for this one."

"Are you serious, Mother? Four bedrooms? Isn't that a lot of room for two people?"

"Well, you won't be two lovebirds for long, unless Amy is just pretending she's pregnant," she said with a smile. "Seriously, there is another part to the proposal. When my grandchild is born, there won't be a spare bedroom for me in this apartment. My gift to myself is a nanny for my grandchild. This is going to sound snooty, and I guess it is: A friend of mine lost her husband of thirty years to cancer. She was an elementary school teacher for twenty-five years. She's looking for a nanny position. I'm asking the two of you to interview her, and, if she's acceptable, hire her for my grandchild's nanny. If you don't think she's a good fit for your family, I have the name of an international nanny placement firm. The nanny would use one of the new bedrooms. The fourth would be reserved for grandparents on both sides."

"I don't know what to say," Reggie said.

"Since Reggie doesn't know what to say, I do: thank you." Amy looked at Reggie and squeezed his hand.

"There is one more issue. Reggie, your father and I are aging and need some help. I don't want to interfere with your careers; however, it would be most helpful if one of you would advise the board of Boykin Enterprises and the other the board of Boykin Properties. It will take minimal time; the boards meet on the second Wednesday of each month. If you agree, we can send the plane for the four of you in the evening before the meeting and fly you back the morning after the meetings."

"The four of us, Mother?"

"Of course. You don't think I'm going to miss a chance to see my grandchild, do you?" Helen smiled. "The advisory fees for the two of you, by chance, happens to equal the cost of whatever nanny you select."

"Father always said you were the brains of the family and very devious. I understand now. We'll have to run it by the partners, but that's just a formality. The fees, however, must be paid to the firm. They'll love getting introduced to the Boykins' contacts in the Midwest."

"Please say yes. Amy, please help me convince Reggie."

"Helen, Reggie will have to make up his own mind; but if he says no, you'll have to help me look for a new husband." The three of them laughed. "Now," Amy said, struggling to get up from the sofa, "why don't we go see this palace you've bought on the twelfth floor?"

1. Amy thought she had it all—a blossoming career and a live-in boyfriend—until she found life throws curves at the most inopportune times. Did Amy handle her situation with Tom well? What would you have done in similar circumstances?

2. Amy's grandmother sheltered her and guided her most of her life. Have you had someone like that in your life? If Amy was your granddaughter, what would you have told her?

3. Reggie Boykin has deep psychological and emotional issues. Amy realized this but didn't know what they were. If you were Amy, given the three options she had, which one would you have chosen?

4. Amy's prized possession is her grandmother's locket. Do you have a special object from a mentor that you feel gives you comfort and helps you cope with decisions?

5. Amy's mother constantly criticizes her. Why? Do you know someone whose parent or relative treats them that way? How do you think Amy should handle the situation?

6. When in the story do you think Amy's feelings for Reggie began changing? When did Reggie's feelings for Amy begin evolving?

7. Why do you think Reggie avoided talking to Amy about Jenny?

8. Is Reggie's attitude realistic toward Amy's pregnancy, as he explains it in the last scene of Chapter 10?

9. Would you want your spouse going on a clothes-buying spree with you?

10. Was it fair or necessary for Reggie to put Amy through the court scene in the judge's chambers? Despite her disappointment and pain from Reggie's actions in the courtroom, Amy wanted to protect him from blame if their charade was discovered. Was this the right perspective?

11. Did Amy handle the confrontation with Isabella well? Would you have done it differently?

12. After dinner at Elio's, Amy could see a bright future and the potential success of the third option. However, she was unaware of the potential disaster ahead of her. Do you know someone who has been through similar circumstances? Do you think Amy was a stronger person at this point?

Acknowledgements

As with many endeavors, several people had a hand in bringing this story to publication.

Luke Palder and his team at Proofreading Services.com did their usual outstanding job of developmental editing, copyediting, and proofreading. Any residual mistakes are mine.

Olivia Hammerman, of Olivia Croom Hammerman Design, LLC, masterfully developed the cover and interior design of the book. Her guidance is appreciated.

Sheree Adams, my assistant for all things digital, kept the logistical work flowing between the various parties in this endeavor.

Judy, my wife, muse, motivator, and best critic read the drafts, discussed clarity, and overall kept me on course to finish the project.

Finally, this novel is all fiction except for Elio's on Second Avenue between 84th and 85th. It is a wonderful restaurant staffed by first class professionals. The food is superb, only outshined by the owner, manager, and staff in the front of the house. If you're in New York, you should make a point of going there.